"You're crazy."

"I'm desperate." Amy looked back at the house again. "Jack, I've felt stuck in this hick town for as long as I can remember." She lifted a hand. "It's my own fault, and I know that. You'd be helping me and I'd be helping you. Win-win."

"So there's nothing here at all?" He moved his finger back and forth, gesturing between the two of them.

She hesitated. "You want the truth or a lie?"

His lips twitched. "The truth, the whole truth, and nothing but the truth."

"The truth is you're a nice guy and a great kisser, but I have bigger fish to fry at the moment. If you're worried about me getting all clingy and having expectations or something...don't."

He sat back. "Brutal honesty. I like it."

"You won't regret it, Jack," she repeated. "You'll see."

He held out his hand. "Should we shake on it?"

Amy peeled off her glove and put her hand in his. The moment their fingers touched sparks zinged up her arm and made her catch her breath. Her gaze rose to Jack's and she saw the same electricity reflected in his pupils.

"It won't get in the way," she assured him.

Dear Reader,

Her Rancher Rescuer marks my very first release for Harlequin American Romance, and the last in the Cadence Creek Cowboys series. Writing it was bittersweet: exciting times are ahead but it's also hard to say goodbye to a series I've loved writing so very much.

I'm really excited to be writing new stories for the Harlequin American Romance line. It's a perfect home for my ranchers and cowboys—strong men and equally strong women working the land and loving hard. But here's something readers might not know. Ever since I sold to Harlequin in 2006, I've been a member of the HMB-Romance author loop, a group specifically set up for authors of the Harlequin Romance line. My only sad thought was that I'd now have to leave that loop behind.

When I said as much to "the girls," it was made very clear that no one would be going anywhere. You see, we're connected by so much more than the lines we write for. We're family. We share our good times and bad, both in the business and in our lives. We trust each other. We love each other. I know for sure they've saved my sanity more than once and I've made friendships that will last a lifetime.

I hope you've enjoyed the Cadence Creek Cowboys series, and you'll follow me to my new home at Harlequin American Romance. We've got some great things planned....

With my very best wishes,

Donna

HER RANCHER RESCUER

DONNA ALWARD

⟨H⟩ **HARLEQUIN**® AMERICAN ROMANCE®

Recycling programs
for this product may
not exist in your area.

ISBN-13: 978-0-373-75506-6

HER RANCHER RESCUER

Copyright © 2014 by Donna Alward

This edition published by arrangement with Harlequin Books S.A.

For questions and comments about the quality of this book, please contact us at CustomerService@Harlequin.com.

Printed in U.S.A.

www.Harlequin.com

ABOUT THE AUTHOR

A busy wife and mother of three (two daughters and the family dog), **Donna Alward** believes hers is the best job in the world: a combination of stay-at-home mom and romance novelist. An avid reader since childhood, Donna has always made up her own stories. She completed her arts degree in English literature in 1994, but it wasn't until 2001 that she penned her first full-length novel and found herself hooked on writing romance. In 2006 she sold her first manuscript, and now writes warm, emotional stories for Harlequin.

In her new home office in Nova Scotia, Donna loves being back on the east coast of Canada after nearly twelve years in Alberta, where her career began, writing about cowboys and the West. Donna's debut romance, *Hired by the Cowboy,* was awarded a Booksellers' Best Award in 2008 for Best Traditional Romance.

With the Atlantic Ocean only minutes from her doorstep, Donna has found a fresh take on life and promises even more great romances in the near future!

Donna loves to hear from readers. You can contact her through her website, www.donnaalward.com, or follow @DonnaAlward on Twitter.

Books by Donna Alward

HARLEQUIN AMERICAN ROMANCE

Dedication

To the girls of the HMB-Romance loop...my writing family no matter where I go. Love you all.

Chapter One

"Amy Wilson is the *last* woman on earth I want to be with."

Amy winced as those words came out of groomsman Rhys Bullock's mouth. He couldn't possibly know she was standing only ten feet behind him, but couldn't he have kept his voice down so the whole guest list at the wedding reception couldn't hear?

The day had been going so well. Callum Shepard's wedding to Avery Spencer had been a gorgeous, Christmassy affair. The food at the golf club was delicious and Amy had been having fun at the dance. Until she'd seen the tension between Rhys and Callum's sister, Taylor. It had been crystal clear to her that they were fighting their attraction. The two of them had been doing a strange mating dance throughout the whole planning of this wedding.

Only minutes ago Amy had caught the bouquet and Rhys the garter. They'd danced and, to her surprise, he'd held her close. But Amy had known exactly what he was thinking—or rather *who* he was thinking about, and it wasn't her. It was as clear as the nose on her face that he belonged with Taylor and Amy had had no illusions as to why Rhys had been so cozy. It had been to make Taylor see what she was missing. Amy had willingly played along, happy to help.

What a fool she'd been to try to steer them in the right direction. She'd known that Rhys didn't like her in *that* way. And neither did she—their one awkward date had proved that months ago. Still, the callousness of the harsh words hurt.

Tears of humiliation sprang to her eyes. But before she could sneak away and pretend she hadn't heard a thing, Rhys and Taylor realized she was standing there. Taylor had the grace to look embarrassed. Of all the Shepard family that Amy had met, Taylor had been the most welcoming. She'd even invited Amy for lunch one day. Now Taylor's pretty face was looking at her with apology etched all over it. Rhys's face was inscrutable, revealing nothing.

"Amy..." Taylor started to apologize but Amy lifted her hand, cutting her off, unable to meet the other woman's sympathetic gaze. This was all embarrassing enough, but she couldn't stand pity. *Poor Amy. Struck out again. Can't hold a man, just like her mother, poor thing.*

Amy's lower lip trembled. She had to get out of here before she really embarrassed herself.

She spun on her heel and made a beeline for the bathroom. One of the stalls was unoccupied and she headed straight for it, going inside and latching the door. She put down the toilet-seat lid, sat down and bit down on her lip. Sometimes she really hated living in this town. Her breakup with Terry years ago had been bad enough. He'd broken her heart and nothing stayed a secret for long in Cadence Creek. Her past relationship with Sam Diamond had been the clincher, though. She'd really liked Sam. She'd been hurt when he'd broken it off and had been a tad too vocal about it.

She knew what people thought of her. A harmless flirt to be gossiped about and laughed at. Looking for love in all the wrong places. Serial dater. She could find a man but not keep a man. She'd heard them all. Besides, no one had forgotten how her dad had just up and left them years before. It had broken her mother. The legacy of his abandonment had followed Amy through to adulthood.

"Who was that?" a woman's voice asked.

A low laugh. "Amy Wilson."

There were a few chuckles. Nothing else had to be said.

She was not a bad person. She didn't sleep around or go after unavailable men. She just…

She just had rotten luck in the romance department. And yet she kept trying and believing that one day the right guy would ride into town and sweep her off her feet. So much so that she knew no one would believe her motives for dancing with Rhys were altruistic, even if she swore it on a Bible. Well, it was the last time she tried to play matchmaker. She might have known it would be misconstrued.

She was done. And the population of Cadence Creek—males *and* females—could dry up and blow away for all she cared.

The door opened and closed again and she held her breath even though she desperately needed a tissue. After a few seconds two tissues appeared over the top of the door. "Here," a man's voice said quietly. "Blow your nose."

"Oh, my God!" Her voice bounced off the porcelain fixtures as she leaped to her feet. "This is the women's room! Get out!"

"I locked the door behind me. Blow your nose, Amy."

She paused. She knew that voice. Not well, which was why it stood out. It was the groom's brother, wasn't it?

Callum's very handsome, very successful younger sibling. "Jack Shepard?"

"Yes, it's me."

"How did you know I was in here?"

He hesitated before answering. "I heard what Rhys said. Saw you take off."

She snagged the tissues from his fingertips and blew her nose—loudly. For another few moments the only sound was the reassuring thump of the DJ's music at the dance, muffled through the walls. "Thanks," she murmured. She and Jack had only bumped into each other a few times. He'd asked her to dance tonight, too. He was a nice guy. But to follow her into the ladies' room? She frowned.

"Are you going to come out of there?" he asked.

"Maybe. When everyone else goes home and I can be humiliated in private." Right now she preferred to lick her wounds in solitude. Gosh, even when she didn't intend to, she found herself in the middle of a spectacle. Memories were too darned long around here. Repetitive.

"It's not even ten o'clock. You could have a long wait."

She hated that he was right. And that he sounded amused. "Then I'll get my coat and slip away. It's not like anyone will miss me."

"Oh, now," he chided, "that sounds a lot like you're going to have your own pity party, and that's no fun."

Right again. He really was being quite annoying. Except he'd come in here to make sure she was okay, *and* he'd given her tissues. She felt herself softening just a little. "Shut up, Jack," she said mildly.

"Who gives a rat's ass what Rhys thinks anyway," Jack suggested. "You're better off without him."

Jack thought this was about Rhys? Of course. Jack was an outsider. Even today, as part of the family, he said and did all the right things but she'd noticed that he'd kept to the side a little bit, included but hovering just on the fringes, not getting too close.

And since he was new here, he definitely didn't understand that the name *Amy Wilson* came with built-in context. "You might want to be careful expressing that opinion," she replied. "Because Rhys has definitely got his eye on your sister."

"I didn't say I didn't like him. I'm just saying that you deserve someone who wants to be with you. Only you. Who can't go on another day without you. Now, are you going to come out of there or not?"

Amy's heart gave an odd thump. What Jack was cavalierly explaining was something she'd felt deep down for a long, long time. She'd always believed *it*—true love— was out there. She'd kept faith that not all guys were losers and deadbeats like her dad. That faith was what kept her from swearing off men. What kept her hoping each time she went on a date. Somewhere out there was someone who would care about her enough to stay.

Problem was, she was starting to think that true love existed all right—but just not for her. That she was somehow inherently flawed. There had to be *some* reason why things never worked out…why all the princes turned out to be frogs. Every relationship attempt had been a disaster. And through it all she'd smiled and tried to pretend it was no big deal. Tried to hide her hurt feelings by moving on….

God, that sounded so desperate.

"I'll come out," she conceded. She stood up and smoothed her dress, a little black number that skimmed her curves and made her feel pretty. Or at least it had. She gave her hair a shake, pasted on a smile. Then and only then did she click back the latch and open the door.

Jack was waiting, looking ridiculously handsome in his tuxedo and boots, the footwear a concession made to a wedding party filled with cowboys. Not a hair on his head was out of place. Jack's features were nearly perfect, except for a small scar just in front of his right ear. He was, she realized, quite dreamy. Except she was giving up all the dreamy nonsense. Especially since Jack was a "here today, gone tomorrow" guy. As soon as the wedding was over it was back to the United States for him, back to running his empire.

"Put some cold water on your face. Touch up your makeup."

She curled her lip at him, taken aback by the blunt orders. "My, aren't we the bossy one."

He shrugged as if he didn't care at all what she thought. "You want to go back out there looking like that?" He pointed at the mirror.

She took a look at herself and frowned. Her eyes were rimmed red, and a bit of mascara had run, leaving black smudges around her lids. Plus she'd either licked or bitten off any remnants of her lipstick.

"Okay, good point." She pulled a piece of paper towel out of the dispenser and turned on the cold water. Jack waited while she dabbed at her eyes, then made short work with a bit of concealer, a touch of mascara and a fresh swipe of gloss across her lips. Not quite flawless, but better.

She turned away from the mirror and faced him. "How's that?"

"Much better."

"Okay. Now I'll go get my coat."

"Really? You're seriously going to run away?"

She raised an eyebrow. What else did he expect her to do? Right now all she wanted was a pint of chocolate fudge ice cream and her fuzzy pajamas. "Yeah, I am. Because I'm sick and tired of being the butt of everyone's… whatever in this town."

"Isn't that a bit overstated?" He gave her a lopsided grin, looking absurdly boyish as he did so.

"Not a bit. I know what people say about me. I can do without a repeat tonight. What Rhys said was quite enough, thanks."

Jack rested his hip on the edge of the counter. "Okay, so help me out here. I don't get it. You're nice, and funny, and pretty easy on the eyes," he said. "Why the gossip?"

She looked away from his intense gaze, touched once more by his compliments. He'd just said she was pretty. Or at least…attractive. "I just don't have a good dating track record. And this damned town is too small. Everyone knows everyone else's business. You screw up once and they remember it *forever*." And sure, she'd screwed up more than once, but had she ever done anything so very bad? No. Still, she was Mary Wilson's daughter. *Like mother like daughter,* the gossipmongers said.

He nodded. "So every date, every failed relationship, every everything is cataloged and talked about?"

She felt her cheeks heat. "In the past I haven't always been…ahem…as discreet as I should have been with my love-life woes."

"You're very self-aware."

Somehow she got the feeling he was teasing her. "I can admit when I make a mistake. For example, I dated Sam Diamond for a while. You've met Sam." Sam was also in the wedding party, along with his brother Tyson. Everyone in Cadence Creek knew Sam Diamond. He headed up Diamondback Ranch now. He was confident and successful and now married to Angela Beck. Even when they'd been dating, Amy had felt he was out of her league.

"Slight age difference?"

She blushed again. "We were both adults. Anyway, when he broke it off I wasn't exactly complimentary about his, er, behavior. I've grown up a bit since then. Doesn't matter, though. I'm painted with a certain brush and that's how I'll always be seen. It's pathetic, really."

"And so you rush off to public bathrooms when your feelings get hurt."

She zipped up her little purse and avoided his eyes. "Ouch, Jack. And I thought you were here to help."

"I am. All I'm saying is that you running in here caused a different sort of scene that put the focus on you and not Rhys."

It bugged her that he was constantly right.

"So what's your brilliant solution?"

He smiled and leaned closer, as if sharing a secret. "The moment I leave this bathroom people are going to think…" He let the thought hang, but it didn't take her long to understand his meaning. They would think that the two of them were locked in there together, doing God knows what.

Her cheeks heated. They would think that she and Jack…that they were… As if her reputation weren't tarnished enough! She pulled back, putting several more inches between them. "Oh, God. They are, aren't they?"

"There's not exactly a back exit or a window to crawl through."

To illustrate his point, the door rattled, and a muffled voice outside said, "It's locked."

"Why did you have to come in here?" She paced in front of the mirror. "I could have just licked my wounds and snuck away." That was her usual M.O., after all.

"Because I was worried about you."

His answer stopped her short. When had anyone really cared about her feelings? "Really?"

"Yes, really."

"Why should you care? You hardly know me."

He nodded. "That's true. But the few times we've been thrown together over the past few weeks, I've enjoyed your company. You're a good dancer."

"A good dancer?" Things were starting to feel a tad bit surreal.

"Yes, and you make me laugh. And I hate it when people aren't treated fairly."

"So you rode to my rescue."

A strange look passed over his face ever so briefly, then was wiped away quickly by another charming smile. "I wouldn't put it that way. I just wanted to make sure you were okay, that's all." He shrugged again. "I guess I didn't think far enough ahead to actually getting you out of this predicament."

It sounded so much like something she'd do that she couldn't help it. She gave a little laugh, putting her fingers to her lips.

The door rattled again and Amy jumped. "You're the genius hotshot. What are we going to do?"

Jack casually put his hands into his pockets as he thought. "Well, if they're going to talk, why don't we give them something to talk about?"

It felt like all the blood that had rushed to her face drained clear out. "If you're proposing that we…in here…" *Oh, my gosh.* While the idea of a romantic interlude with Jack Shepard was more than intriguing, she wasn't prepared for *that.* She didn't do those sorts of things despite what people might think. Jack was a man of the world. He probably had women falling all over him all the time.

World-class athlete turned business mogul? Yeah. And it wasn't like she was a prude, but it was a long jump to hookup sex in a public bathroom.

He chuckled. "No, not that. Though to be honest it's an alluring idea. What I meant was, come back to the dance. Dance with me again to show everyone it doesn't matter. And then I'll drive you home."

That she didn't dismiss the idea right away spoke volumes. Could she do it? Walk out of here with her head held high and ignore all the whispers? A little part of her said that she was treated the way she was because she perpetuated the perception. Why did everyone's opinion of her matter so much, anyway?

No one would be expecting a strong, confident woman who didn't give a damn. And she really wanted to be that woman for once in her life.

"We already danced twice," he reminded her. "Spent time in a locked bathroom. All that will happen is that they'll keep on believing what they already think to be true. And would that be so bad?"

"That I'm a chaser and a…"

Frowning, he put a finger over her lips. "Don't say that word. Just don't. You're not."

His finger was warm and firm against the soft flesh of her lips and for a long moment their gazes caught and held. He didn't like what she'd been about to say. She wondered why. Wondered if he really did have a rescue complex. There had to be a flaw somewhere. Jack Shepard was just a little too perfect.

"Come dance with me. Otherwise you're just running with your tail between your legs. I don't know about you, but I've always preferred a good fight to a quiet retreat."

Easy for him to say. She'd be here in town long after he was gone. She'd be the one going to a bleak and dis-

mal home night after night when what she really longed
for was some color and excitement. With a sinking heart,
she realized tonight would only be more ammunition
for those people who would make her a laughingstock.

She remembered the news reports in the sports pages
after Jack's ski injury. They hadn't always been kind.
They'd said something like "Fast on *and* off the hill."
Jack had faced a fair bit of nasty press in his day but
he'd risen above it. She could do worse for a champion,
she supposed.

And then there were Callum and Avery, the bride and
groom, and Jack's sister, Taylor, who'd been surprisingly
nice to her at Avery's wedding shower. And her boss, Melissa Stone, who'd given her a chance with her job. She
was pretty sure that working with Melissa had snagged
her the invite to the wedding in the first place.

But could she do it? Could she face them all with her
head held high? It was a tall order, when she'd been aware
of the whispers for years. Since she was ten and her dad
had walked out. She'd heard the rumors that he'd left
them for someone else. Had no idea if they were true or
not, because her mother wouldn't speak of him.

"That's a crazy idea." She still had the urge to collect
her coat and flee. It would be easier....

"Probably. But if you run away, they win."

And then he smiled, a conspiratorial sort of grin that
climbed his cheek and warmed the depths of his eyes.
Like they were in cahoots. And in that moment Amy realized that she didn't just think Jack was okay. She really, truly liked him. He would be a good person to have
on her side.

Her heartbeat quickened with nerves. "One dance, and
then you'll take me home?"

"Cross my heart." He made the motion over his left breast and then held out his hand. "Shall we?"

She swallowed tightly, her throat constricting as she braced herself for whatever was on the other side of the door. "I'm game if you are." The words sounded more sure than she really was.

She put her fingers in his and squeezed. Lifted her chin and shook her hair back over her shoulders. He returned the squeeze of her fingers, giving her confidence. She took a deep breath, let it out slowly.

Amy refused to look anywhere but straight ahead as Jack unlocked the door and swung it open. Half a dozen people were standing around, and out of the corner of her eye she saw someone from the club maintenance crew coming around the corner—presumably to unlock the locked door. She felt heat climb her cheeks but then Jack squeezed her hand reassuringly.

"Hey, how's it going?" he asked the room at large, tugging her behind him. She gaped. How could he sound so casual? So effortlessly charming? She hurried to keep up with him, which was difficult considering his long legs and her high heels. She could feel the stares on her back and had the oddest urge to giggle. Considering all the times she hadn't wanted to make a spectacle and had anyway, this moment was surreal and more than a little comical. She'd pegged Jack as a lot of things—handsome, charming—but she hadn't considered him chivalrous. There really was no other way to describe his actions tonight.

She got her footing and evened out her stride, keeping her chin defiantly raised. Jack was right. This felt much better than slinking away as if she were guilty of something! The only thing she was guilty of was trying to help.

The song playing was a fast one, so Jack steered her

toward the bar first. "Tonic and lime for me, champagne for the lady, please," he ordered, and in seconds a glass of fizz was placed in her hand. "Cheers," he said, touching his glass to hers. "Come on."

He took her hand again and led her to the fringe of the floor. They paused and she took a long drink of champagne, enjoying the bubbles as they exploded on her tongue. The last time she'd had champagne it wasn't real champagne at all but the cheap fizzy stuff from the liquor store that cost less than ten dollars a bottle and was far too sweet. This was drier, with a bit of bite, and tasted expensive.

And just like that she was reminded once more that Jack Shepard was a millionaire. Maybe even a billionaire. Not that he put on airs or anything, or threw his money around. It was easy to forget when he was here, in a place like this, dressed like all the other groomsmen. Truth be told, on a regular day 90 percent of the guys here would be in boots and Stetsons. Jack's sporting goods empire was huge and he ran some sort of outdoor adventure ranch in Montana. He'd been an Olympic downhiller, just missing the podium in his one and only games before going on to make his mark in the business world. And she'd been locked in a bathroom with him for a good ten, fifteen minutes.

The nervous giggle she'd been holding in slipped out.

"What's so funny?"

"Nothing," she answered, draining her glass of champagne and looking longingly at the empty flute. It would be gauche to ask for another, but oh, my, it was delicious.

She noticed Jack give a nod to the DJ, and seconds later the song changed to something slower.

He took her hand and led her to the floor. His fingers gripped hers, his other hand placed firmly on the hollow of her back as he drew her close. In her heels, she only had to tip her head a little to have her lips at the bottom of his ear. "You *are* used to people taking your orders," she observed as their feet began to move.

"Yes, I am. But only when I'm being reasonable."

"Are you ever unreasonable?"

He lowered his chin and looked down at her, his expression unexpectedly serious. "Not as often as I used to be."

Something delicious swirled around in her tummy. "You mean you've left your bad-boy days behind?"

"Mostly."

She blinked. "Mostly?" What did that mean?

"Well, locking myself in a bathroom with you probably wasn't the most reasonable move. Though I must say I did behave myself. Even you can't deny that."

She was about to laugh when he said, "More's the pity."

And the laugh died in her throat, replaced instead by an acute awareness of what could have happened in that bathroom. What everyone probably thought had happened....

"They were going to talk regardless," he said quietly, his lips against her temple as he read her thoughts. "This way they talk about you sneaking away with me instead of locking yourself away crying over him."

He was right. And she would rather that, than everyone view her as pathetic, as they normally did.

As his hand rode perilously close to her tailbone, she recalled the scandal that broke just prior to the fall that messed up his knee for good. There'd been a photograph of him and a woman.... His coach's wife, if she remembered correctly. Had he been in love with her? Licked his wounds in private? What secrets was Jack hiding beneath his cool, confident exterior? There had to be more to the man than what she saw. No one was *that* perfect.

"Do you love him, Amy?"

"What? Who?" she asked, confused.

They danced along to the music, feet moving in perfect rhythm. "Rhys Bullock. Are you in love with him?"

"God, no." The denial came swiftly to her lips. Rhys was attractive, and for most of the women in Cadence Creek, the ungettable get. They'd gone on exactly one date and while he was nice enough, they hadn't clicked at all. Catching the bouquet had been pure chance. And Rhys hadn't exactly pushed her away during the dance. Rhys was a challenge to the female population of Cadence Creek.

"Then why the tears?" Jack asked.

She met his gaze. "Truthfully? Humiliation. It's not every day that someone claims you're the last woman on earth they'd want to date. Now be quiet, eh? I have a lot more fun when we're not talking."

His eyes flashed at her. "Be careful, talking like that could get you into trouble."

"You promised to be honorable."

"I still have to drive you home. The night's not over yet."

Again, the curl of excitement wound through her as he flirted. She was under no illusions. There was no future with Jack. He was not a romantic prospect or a ticket anywhere, nor did she want him to be. But he was fun and interesting and different and exciting, and at this moment those were fantastic attributes. It beat the hell out of chocolate fudge ice cream and a ten-year-old chick flick on cable.

His arm tightened around her, pulling her closer against his length. He still wore his tuxedo jacket, unbuttoned, and her fingers pressed against the rich, thick material. She slipped her fingers beneath the lapel and felt the heat of his skin through the satiny material of his vest. "You have a lot of layers on," she murmured, her lashes fluttering as the hand at her waist kneaded the top of her tailbone.

She was deliberately tempting him. After they'd already set out the ground rules.

"Say the word and they're gone," he answered, calling her bluff.

She kept silent.

"This is a killer dress," he commented. "*Little black dress* sounds so simple. But it's not simple on you."

"Is there a motive behind your compliments? Or are you just keeping up the charade?"

"It's the truth. You look beautiful tonight. The men of this town must all be blind if they can't see it."

She shrugged. "I've lived here all my life. I'm not a novelty."

"They're blind *and* stupid, then."

She smiled. "You're doing a good job, anyway."

"A good job?"

"Of turning the situation around and puffing up my ego. You were right. A dance was a better idea than running off with my tail between my legs."

"We only forgot one thing."

"We did?"

"Well, yes. If you want everyone to believe you don't give a damn about Rhys."

Curious, she tilted her head up to meet his gaze. Suddenly she couldn't hear the music, couldn't see the other partygoers around them. She was oblivious to everything but Jack. The way he looked, all suave and debonair with his dark hair and bedroom eyes and broad shoulders. But more than that was the way he was looking at her. Like she was the only woman in the world. No one had ever, ever looked at her that way.

It seemed the most obvious thing for a kiss to be the next step. They slid into it naturally, like they'd done it a thousand times before. Her head tilted slightly to the left, there was a first meeting of lips, then they opened a little wider as they tasted and explored. It felt strangely familiar and yet somehow brand-new. They kept it light, kept their hands where they belonged, especially considering they were in public. But it was a hell of a kiss all the same—the kind of kiss that made her toes curl in her platform pumps and goose bumps shiver over her skin. And when it was over her breath was coming a little bit faster than before. *Wow.*

"If there were ever any doubt…" he said, putting the final bow on the top by touching his lips to her temple in a tender and intimate gesture.

But his words made Amy go suddenly cold, like she was splashed with icy water. This wasn't real. It was an act, a performance. A charity service. It was all about perception. Showing the town that she didn't give a damn about Rhys Bullock and his insults.

"What's wrong?"

"Nothing."

But Jack was smart. Especially for a guy. He squeezed her hand to get her attention. "You think because we let them see what we wanted them to see that it wasn't real."

"What a charming way you have with words," she replied drily, her gaze sliding away.

"You think it was an act."

"Wasn't it? A lovely stage for me to save face for a few minutes. What's in it for you, Jack? Something to keep you from being bored?"

His jaw tightened. Had she struck a nerve?

"Would that be so bad?"

She hated that the immediate answer that came back to her was no. The problem was there was no excitement in Cadence Creek. No adventure or challenge. It was always the same, day in and day out. She longed to get out, but every time she thought of escaping she thought of leaving her mother alone and couldn't quite do it. As much as she got frustrated with her mom, she worried about her. Amy was sure Mary was depressed. And she hardly ever went out.... How could Amy possibly leave her to fend for herself?

"Well, it's humiliation of a different sort."

"News flash," he said in a low voice. "Being with you is a great distraction. There are far worse things than holding a beautiful woman in your arms."

"That might be nice if I thought you meant it."

A wrinkle formed between his eyebrows as he frowned. "Amy, we danced twice tonight already. It was fun. There was eye contact and we flirted. Did it occur to you that maybe I didn't like the thought of someone like you being in that bathroom crying over some guy who's not worth it?"

"No."

"*No* what?"

"No, it didn't occur to me."

"Why?"

"Because in my experience most guys don't give a good damn about my feelings."

"Then you've been hanging around the wrong men."

"No," she corrected, suddenly feeling like telling the absolute truth. "It's me. I'm messed up and guys try to stay away from that kind of crazy."

She was surprised when he burst out laughing. "What's so funny?" she asked.

He looked down at her warmly. With—she would swear—affection. "Amy, I used to hurl myself down the side of a mountain at over eighty miles an hour. I *like* crazy. Besides, I don't think you're crazy at all. Misunderstood, maybe. But not crazy."

That he could be so astute momentarily silenced her. The music faded and he moved his hand at her back, letting her go but still holding tightly to her right hand. "Are you ready to go now, or would you like to stay a little longer?"

She looked around. A few faces were staring in their direction, but not all. Some were at the bar, some were in groups talking, others were taking to the dance floor. The truth was she was tired of them all. All the familiar faces, all people who knew—or thought they knew—far too much about her. She couldn't wait to get out of here. "I'm ready. My coat's at the check."

"You get it and I'll join you in a moment. I'm just going to say goodbye to Callum and Avery."

Of course. The bride and groom. His brother and new sister-in-law. Ignoring anyone who might want to speak to her, she made straight for the coat check. She was just tying the belt of her coat when Jack came up beside her, holding a bottle of champagne in his hand. "What are you...?"

He got his coat, tipped the coat-check girl and put a hand on her elbow. "I got the impression you liked the champagne."

She couldn't lie. "I did."

"And that you might just happen to like me a little bit."

"You're not exactly a troll."

He chuckled and opened the door to the outside. The

frigid wind blasted against her, eating through the thin material of her stockings. He put his free arm around her and bundled her close as he led her across the parking lot to his rented car. "So leaving the dance doesn't mean having to say good-night. I swiped a bottle from the bar. Come back to the B and B with me."

Chapter Two

The B and B. Amy wasn't exactly sure how much privacy they'd have there. And then there was the matter of what Jack expected out of tonight. She was tempted. Oh, so tempted. But she wasn't the kind to spend a night in a man's hotel room. Especially one she barely knew. She was more on the fairy-tale end of the spectrum when it came to romance, and not the fast and loose.

He opened her door and helped her inside, then jogged around the hood and got in, turned on the engine and let it warm up. It was better out of the wind but still cold, and she wished the heater would kick in.

"I don't think this is a good idea," she said, regretting having to say the words but determined to make a smart decision for once in her life.

"Why not?"

"For exactly the same reason nothing happened in the ladies' room."

"You're not the casual-sex type."

"You're a risk taker. I'm not." Even if at times she rather wished she was…. Maybe she would have let Cadence Creek see the back of her long before now. Some days she worried she was turning out more and more like her mother. Afraid. Stuck in a rut and never strong enough to get out. God, she hoped she wasn't that person.

Heat began to surround her feet. Jack rubbed his hands together. "No sex," he said. "I'll make a solemn promise that this is not a hookup type of proposition."

She tilted her head as she looked at him. "Then why? I mean…what's in it for you?"

Their gazes locked for a few seconds and then he looked away. "Honestly? I'm looking forward to taking off this jacket and tie and just hanging out for a while. Not being 'Jack, the Groom's Brother,' who says and does all the right things."

Surprise rippled through her. Maybe Perfect Jack was just an act? Or at least covering the real Jack…. And boy, oh, boy, could she understand that.

"Look," he said, "just come back, have a glass of champagne with me. I was on chauffeur duty today and abstained all night. We can just chill and then I'll walk you home." He gazed at her sharply. "You do live within walking distance, right?"

"Just off of Main, on Maple."

"Scout's honor, Amy. We won't do anything you don't want to do."

That was just the problem. She didn't know what she wanted. And if she had some of that champagne, she wasn't sure how much willpower she'd have to turn away a man like Jack Shepard. The kiss on the dance floor was still front and center in her mind.

"An hour," she finally said. "That's all. An hour and a glass of champagne and then I go home and you go back to…"

Gosh, she didn't even really know where he called home, did she?

"To my ranch in Montana."

Montana. One summer she and her mother had taken a trip across the border through Glacier Park and spent a few days in Kalispell. It had been beautiful. They'd driven past this resort-type place that was huge, and she'd wondered what it would be like to stay there, order room service and look out at the mountains. Instead they'd gotten a room at a nationwide discount chain. It had still been fun, but even then, Amy had wanted more.

"I suppose you have a huge place there," she said, blowing on her fingers as he drove out of the lot.

"It's a working ranch. I bought it a few years ago with the idea of turning it into a corporate retreat. I spent some time in the area on vacation and really enjoyed the physical challenges, so I flew in my whole management team and we did this week-long team-building thing. It was so much fun I decided to have a go at it myself." He smiled. "Now I consider it home. I still keep an apartment in Vancouver, but I'm not there much. Turns out I'm not much of a city guy when all is said and done."

Jack was different when he talked about his ranch, more relaxed, animated. She got the feeling that this was closer to the real Jack than the man who had ridden to her rescue in the ladies' bathroom.

"Do you wear the boots and hat and the whole nine yards?"

He laughed. "Of course. All our cattle work is done on horseback. We do a few drives during the year, not to mention the trail rides."

She sighed. Just when she thought how different he was from the men she knew, it turned out he was the same, after all. After living her whole life in Cadence Creek, she was a little tired of the whole cowboy scene.

It took hardly any time to reach the town, and with a few quick turns Jack pulled up in front of the B and B. He grabbed the champagne and came around and opened her door, offering her his free hand.

The owners had gone to bed but Jack's parents, Susan and Harry, sat up in the parlor, quietly talking and enjoying a glass of wine. Amy felt her face twist into a guilty expression the moment they stepped into the room.

"Jack, dear." Susan suddenly noticed Amy behind him. "Oh, hello."

"Hello, Mrs. Shepard."

Parents were not part of the plan. This was the worst idea ever. She should never have gone along with it.

Jack put the champagne bottle down onto a side table and began unbuttoning his overcoat. "It's a cold one. I invited Amy back for a drink. I hope that's okay. Both of us were getting a little tired of the festivities."

"Of course. We were just heading to bed...."

Harry's brows were slightly raised, inquisitive. Jack grinned. "Why don't you stay up and have a glass of champagne with us? It would give us all some time to just hang out and chill. It's been a crazy few days."

Harry nodded, as if satisfied. "Yes, it has. Your mother and I had quite a job getting Nell down for the night." He nodded at a baby monitor beside him. "I wouldn't say no to champagne. You open it while I grab some glasses, Jack. Kathleen showed me where she keeps them."

While the men got the drinks, Amy took off her coat and hung it up on the antique coatrack in the corner, nerves tumbling around in her stomach. She'd met the Shepard children during the wedding planning, but she'd only really seen Mr. and Mrs. Shepard from a distance. Now she knew where Jack got his aura of success and Taylor got her class. It was intimidating as hell. "It was a lovely wedding," she said to Susan, scrambling for something to say.

"Yes, it was. If I remember right, you work at the flower shop, yes?"

"I do, yes."

"The flowers were beautiful. You did a great job."

If nothing else, Mrs. Shepard was trying to be nice. "Melissa does all the designing. Though she has shown me how to do some simple arrangements."

"Do you like it there?"

Amy shrugged. "It's okay." She smiled. "I actually like the business side of it better, but it's a small shop. Know what I mean?"

Susan smiled. "Actually, I do. Not enough challenge to keep you going."

"That's it exactly." Amy smiled. Jack's parents weren't anywhere near as intimidating as she expected. At least his mother wasn't. Harry Shepard carried a distinct air of authority.

There was a loud pop and then glasses were filled. To Amy's surprise, she and Jack sat on the sofa together and everyone simply chatted—about the wedding, about Cadence Creek, about Callum and Avery's daughter, Nell. Clearly the elder Shepards were enjoying being grandparents. Finally Susan stifled a yawn. "Oh, my goodness. I think it's time I went to bed. We've got to be up with the baby in the morning, and to see Callum and Avery off on their honeymoon."

She stood and came to Jack, who also stood for a hug. "It was good spending some extra time with you, sweetheart. We don't see you enough."

"I know." He grinned at her crookedly. "You should come down to the ranch for a week. I'll take you ziplining."

Harry chuckled. "Maybe we will. I'd like to see your mother on one of those contraptions. Good night, son. And you, too, Amy. It was nice to meet you."

"Nice to meet you, too," she said, and meant it.

They hadn't spent an hour sipping bubbly in Jack's room, but in some ways this had been better. She'd felt welcomed and relaxed. It was, to her surprise, the perfect ending to the day.

They said their good-nights and Jack turned to her. "I suppose this is where I say I should walk you home," he said.

"I suppose it is." She stood and put her glass down onto a coffee table. "I'll get my coat."

"Not so fast," he murmured, catching her hand when she would have turned away. He pulled her back so that she was in front of him. He put his hand at her waist, his fingers sliding along the soft material of the curve-hugging dress. "I was on my best behavior," he murmured, his voice low and intimate. "I kept my promise, too. The least you can do is give me a kiss good-night."

"I suppose it is only fair." She smiled up at him. If nothing else, in the past few hours Jack had given her something that she hadn't had in a very long time: acceptance. She hadn't felt the need to be anyone other than who she was. Hadn't felt pressed to meet any sort of expectation. Perhaps that was because the Shepards hadn't been in Cadence Creek very long. Or perhaps it was because they were a genuinely nice, normal family.

And after tonight it was unlikely she'd ever even see Jack again. The least she could do was take a kiss to remember him by.

She tilted her face up and kissed him, and with far less reserve than she'd shown on the dance floor. His arms came around her and pulled her close; she twined hers around his neck and slid her fingers through his hair. They were as close as two people could be with their clothes on, pressed together at several contact points. Jack's hands roved over her back and came to tangle in her long curls as he tilted her head back and took command of her mouth. He tasted like man and the rich, erotic tang of champagne.

If he asked, she realized, she might reconsider her earlier bargain.

"Do you know how beautiful you are?" he asked roughly. "If I didn't have to leave tomorrow night, I think I'd actually consider seeing where this leads."

"But you are leaving tomorrow night."

"Yes." He nibbled at her earlobe and her eyes rolled back in her head with pleasure.

"And you're not coming back."

"Well," he said, and he kissed her neck just below her ear, "I'm back on Christmas Eve and gone again Boxing Day."

"And spending it with your family."

"Yeah."

They kissed a little longer until they were both out of breath.

"Jack, you should take me home. This would be a foolish mistake."

She stepped backward, her chest rising and falling with exertion, her body humming with arousal. Of all the times to be sensible…and yet she was somehow happy about her choice. She was nearly twenty-five. It was time she took control of her life rather than simply letting it happen to her, time she decided what it was she wanted and found a way to get it. She could start by not letting herself get swept away in a moment that would only be a dead end.

She'd figure the rest out in time. Changing your life was a big job for one night.

"You're right. I'll get our coats." He stepped back and

ran a hand through his hair. "But dammit, Amy, you are not an easy woman to walk away from."

As he disappeared around the corner toward the foyer, Amy bit down on her lip and blinked a few times. Jack couldn't possibly know that that was the sweetest thing he could have said to her tonight.

AMY COULDN'T STAND being in the house another moment.

It was Christmas Eve. It should have been a time for happiness and joy and presents and carols and hot chocolate spiked with peppermint schnapps. Instead there wasn't even a tree up at her house. A little-known secret— if Cadence Creek had any secrets—was that Christmas simply didn't happen at the Wilson house in any way, shape or form. Not since she was ten years old and her dad had walked out on her and her mother on December twenty-third. Neither of them had seen him since.

It made Amy bitter. Naturally it had ruined that Christmas, but she didn't see why it had to ruin every holiday since. But her mother was adamant. No tree. No turkey dinner, no *Miracle on 34th Street*.

As much as she understood, Amy refused to be Scrooged out of the holiday altogether. Tonight she would sing carols and look at the tree decorated at the front of the sanctuary and soak it all in for a blessed hour. She looked forward to this every year.

"Mom, why don't you come with me? The service is so great."

"Not this year, Amy." Mary Wilson's voice was tired. She looked up from her chair, where she was watching television. "You go and have fun."

Amy went back into the living room and perched on the arm of the sofa. Since the wedding she'd been doing a lot of thinking. Thinking about what she wanted and the person she wanted to be. Something had changed in the moment she'd stepped out of the bathroom with Jack. Something good. Something…strong.

She'd been going to wait to broach the subject but the time felt right. "Mom, what would you say if I told you I wanted to go to school?"

Mary's head turned, her program forgotten. "School? When? Where?" Was that fear Amy saw in her eyes? It only made her more nervous. Amy kept pushing for Mary to get out, but what would happen if she weren't here anymore to give that nudge?

"Not far," Amy assured her. "In the fall. I've been looking into college courses in the city. I'd have to get an apartment, but I wouldn't be far away. I could come home lots. Every weekend."

She wished she could tell what her mother was thinking. But years of hiding her emotions had served Mary well. Her face gave away nothing now that the initial shock was over. "You're unhappy at the flower shop?" Mary asked.

Amy chose her words carefully. She didn't want to put everything on her mother's shoulders. It wasn't about blame, though Amy did harbor some resentment for how she'd grown up in a cheerless house. At the same time, she understood. And she would never, ever want to add to her mom's distress.

"I just can't see myself staying there for the rest of my life, you know? I want more. I want…options. But I don't want to leave you all alone, either."

"Don't worry about me."

Amy frowned. "But I do worry about you. About you being alone. I wish you'd come with me to church. Maybe try to be a part of the community again. Don't you think it's time?"

Mary looked away. "Maybe another time. Just not today."

Amy knew that look. It was the "discussion closed" look. Disappointed, she got up. "I won't be too late," she said quietly.

"Have a good time."

The words sounded empty. There was no joy at Christmas, not in the Wilson house. And while Amy longed to get away, she was worried, too. Worried about what would happen to her mom if she were left all alone. At least now she left the house to work. Get groceries. What if that changed?

Amy walked to the church, taking deep breaths of the cold air and enjoying the sound of snow crunching under her favorite boots to shake her dull mood. The parking lot was already full and golden light spilled from the windows, welcoming her. She shook off the heavy weight of her talk with her mom and stepped inside into the warmth and cheer.

Then she spotted Jack.

He'd really come back to celebrate Christmas with his family, then. Something warm and lovely wound its way through her, making her smile. Jack had been a wonderful surprise at the wedding. She'd been at her lowest in the moment Rhys had uttered those words. To her it hadn't felt like she was the last woman *he* wanted to be with—it had felt like she was the last woman *anyone* would want. That she had absolutely nothing to offer.

Jack had changed that. Oddly enough it hadn't been his attention that had affected her so deeply. Or the way he'd kissed her and held her close—though that had been very memorable. It was how he'd brought her in, included her in his evening with his parents. As if she belonged. As if she were their equal. She'd never had that before.

He looked over and his face broke out in a smile when he recognized her. She gave a little wave and watched as he excused himself from the group he was in and came over.

"Hey," he said, and to her surprise he gave her a quick hug. He smelled scrumptious, some sort of expensive cologne she didn't recognize. "I wasn't expecting to see you tonight."

"Just about the whole town goes out for the local services," she replied. "I wouldn't miss it."

"You're here alone?"

She shrugged, trying to look nonchalant. "My mom's the exception to the rule. Long story."

"You'll sit with us, then." He said it as if it were a done deal.

"Jack, you don't have to do that. I'm a big girl." She batted her eyelashes. "See? No tears. No rescuing of damsels in distress required tonight."

Once again that strange expression washed over his face, but then he smiled brightly at her. "Well, that's good news. But you can sit with us anyway." He leaned in. "I'm the only one not paired up. I hate being a third wheel."

She doubted that but it was also nice to know she didn't have to sit alone. "Okay, then."

"Let me hang up your coat."

She grinned at him. "Are you trying to start more rumors?"

He laughed. "My mom taught me good manners, remember?"

"I'll remember to thank her for it later."

He took the coat from her hands and hooked it on a hanger. "So…how've you been?"

"Good," she answered. "Busy." It was true. The flower shop had been steady all week long. "Doing some thinking."

"Oh, that sounds interesting." He raised an eyebrow.

"I came to a rather radical decision, actually. I need to get out of here, Jack. What am I going to do, work at the flower shop for the rest of my life?"

"You're getting itchy feet?"

She nodded. "I want to *do* something. I want to see places. So I'm taking the next eight months to build up my savings so I can move to the city and take classes when the fall term starts."

They made their way slowly to the sanctuary door. "That's great, Amy. Any idea what you're going to study?"

She nodded. "Hospitality management. I like working with people. And I have good organizational skills. I think I could be good at it."

"I can see that. You're very good at the flower shop." He stared at her for a few moments more and she wondered what he was thinking. She also noticed shadows beneath his eyes. Jack, for all his charming smiles, was exhausted. What was causing him to lose sleep?

"You don't think I can do it?" she asked.

"On the contrary. Didn't I just say so?"

The words were glib but there was an edge to his voice that confirmed her suspicion. "Hey, is everything okay with you? You look tired. A little stressed."

"Funny you should mention that…"

At that moment his family made their way over and suggested they find their seats, so their conversation was halted until they found themselves packed into a rather full pew. She didn't mind being close to Jack. In fact she'd thought about it perhaps a little too often over the past several days.

"Where's Taylor?" Amy asked, opening the bulletin and scanning the order of service.

"We had dinner at the diner. I think she stayed to help Rhys and Martha clean up."

"They're still an item, then?"

He nudged her with his elbow. "You've been here all week. You'd know better than I would."

She turned her head and met his gaze. "I've been avoiding the gossip mill. And from the look on your face, I'd say you know more than you're letting on. Anyway, I was just making conversation."

Jack sighed. "Sorry. You were right before. I'm touchy."

"Any reason in particular?" She put down the bulletin and gave him her full attention.

"Labor issues. Or rather, lack of. One of my staff was in a bad accident this week."

Amy put her hand on his arm. "Oh, no! Are they okay?"

He nodded. "Yes, thank goodness. Or she will be—in time. But it was serious. She's got a broken pelvis, and the doctors say that she'll be off at least three months."

"Surely someone can fill in for her? A temp?"

Jack shook his head. "She basically runs the corporate retreat business at the ranch. I did what I could this week while I was there, but on Boxing Day I'm going back there again to get things settled. Once the holidays are over, we've got groups starting up again. Groups that have been booked for months. Finding a temp this week, with all the statutory holidays? Just about impossible."

The service started and the lights dimmed. After several carols to set the mood, there was a brief message and then came Amy's favorite part—"Silent Night." Everyone was given a single candle in a holder, and as the choir started the first verse, the minister made his way down the aisle and lit the candles on the end. Wick was touched to wick until all the candles were lit and the congregation joined in for the second and third verses.

Beside her, Jack relaxed, his warm, tenor voice joining in with the others.

And then it was over, the candles extinguished, and the lights came up. Chatter erupted as good wishes for the holiday were exchanged. Little children bounced with excitement, because now that church was over they were one step closer to Santa Claus. Jack chuckled as one particularly cute boy with little round glasses tugged on his father's hand, claiming they had to hurry and get the cookies out so he could go to bed.

"Amy, good to see you again." Susan came over and gave her a brief hug. "Do you have plans for the holiday?"

Once she got over the surprise of the affectionate gesture, Amy smiled. "Oh, just spending tomorrow with my mom. Keeping things quiet."

"That sounds lovely."

Callum and Avery joined them briefly, Callum carrying a sleeping Nell. "Merry Christmas, Amy."

"You, too. Baby's first Christmas. Pretty exciting at your house."

"Yeah." Avery smiled. "And it's nice to have all of Callum's family here. I see Taylor and Rhys made it." She nodded toward the back of the church, where the couple was standing with Rhys's mother, Martha.

To Amy's mind, the way Avery paired their names together pretty much answered any question Jack might have had.

Jack turned to Amy. "How'd you get here?"

She smiled. "I walked. Got some fresh air."

"I'll drive you home."

"Are you sure?"

He smiled back. "Of course I am. I do know where you live."

Yes, he did. He'd walked her home before in the cold.

Any lingering they might have done at her door had been cut short by the frigid wind and her freezing feet. But it hadn't stopped him from leaning in and dropping a light kiss on her lips just the same.

They gathered their coats and he led her to his new rental car.

The heater hadn't even really kicked in by the time they got to her house. Jack parked on the street and left the engine running. "I wish I could see you again before I go back, but with family obligations and the trouble back home…"

"I understand completely. It's no biggie, Jack. I didn't even think I'd see you again. Thanks for including me tonight."

"I was glad for the company."

"So you're heading back on the twenty-sixth. Any idea what you're going to do about your problem?"

He sighed. "Making sure Rosa's doing okay and that her family has everything they need is the first thing. And then I'll have to check I have the bookings straight and look at hiring someone to fill in."

"Surely it won't be that difficult. Is there an agency you can use?"

"Maybe, but Rosa's a force of nature. She looks after the business but also does all the cooking and cleaning for our guests. I'll probably have to hire two people to replace her."

Amy looked out the window. A flurry was starting, little white flakes drifting to the ground. All along her street houses were lit up with lights—white ones, multicolored, inflatable snowmen and penguins—and every door held a wreath. But not hers. There was a glow from a single window but no flickering reflection of a Christmas tree or any hint of holiday cheer. She didn't want to go inside. Wished she could be anywhere but here right now. Then felt automatically guilty about it.

"My mom's not much for decorating," she said quietly, knowing Jack had to have noticed.

"And you never thought to go about it yourself?"

She looked over at him. His features were illuminated by the dashboard lights. There was no criticism in his voice. In fact, Jack Shepard was probably the first person she'd ever met who didn't seem to make any judgments at all. Maybe he'd been on the receiving end and knew how it felt. Once again she remembered the stories from the news. Speculation about the affair right under his coach's nose. How much of it had been true? It was hard to believe he would have done such a thing. It just wasn't *Jack*.

"My mom forbade decorating," she answered, her voice barely above a whisper. "My dad left us at Christmas. She hates the holidays."

"I'm sorry. That's rough."

"It was years ago. She should be able to move on. But moving on seems to be one thing neither of us are very good at. I swear, Jack, deciding to go away to school has taken such a load off my shoulders. And yet…"

"And yet she'll be here alone. And you'll worry about her."

"Yeah," she answered, relieved he understood.

He reached over and took her hand. "Do you want to come over to Callum's tomorrow? I'm sure it would be fine with Avery."

"No, that's okay. I just wish…"

"You wish what?"

She sighed. "That I could get away for a bit. Just somewhere different, to really think about what it is I want."

"Where you won't be influenced one way or the other?"

"Or fall back into comfortable habits."

Her gaze met his as a kernel of an idea took hold. He had a problem, and she was restless. What if they could help each other out?

"Look, things around the shop are always slow after Christmas. What if…" She took a deep breath. "What if I came down and helped you out for a few weeks? I'm pretty sure I could handle the admin you need done. It'd give you some breathing room before having to hire someone new."

"You're serious."

"Of course I'm serious. It would only be for a short time." Her mom would be fine for a few weeks. It would be a good trial run.

He turned in the seat and faced her squarely. "I couldn't officially pay you, you understand. Unless you have a U.S. work visa I know nothing about."

He was considering it. She didn't mind the work; she could file and type and answer phones and schedule things without blinking an eye. In return she'd have a few weeks in a Montana lodge, surrounded by snow and roaring fires and whatever else she could come up with. "It'd be like a vacation for me, I promise. You don't have to pay me anything. I'll do it in exchange for room and board."

"You're crazy."

"I'm desperate." She looked back at the house again. "Jack, I've felt stuck in this hick town for as long as I can remember." She lifted a hand. "It's my own fault, and I know that. You'd be helping me and I'd be helping you. Win-win."

"I'm not sure desperation is the best motive here."

Was he talking about her need to get away or the small matter of what had happened between them less than two weeks ago? They'd been all but plastered together on the dance floor and later in the parlor at the B and B. She wasn't sure how to bring it up, but she felt one of them should.

"If you're worried about there being *atmosphere,* don't. That's not why I'm going. I've sworn off men, remember?"

He laughed shortly. "I've heard that before."

She put her hand on his arm. Even through his overcoat she felt the strength and warmth of it. There was no denying that Jack was strong and sexy as hell. No denying that her pulse had raced being held in his arms. But for once in her life she was focused on a goal. She wasn't about to get distracted now. Not even by someone as amazing as Jack.

"It would be good experience for me. If I'm considering going into hospitality management, what better training could I ask for? If I like it I'll be really sure. And it'll be a good test run for my mom, too. It'll take her some getting used to—being alone, that is."

"So there's nothing here at all?" He moved his finger back and forth, gesturing between the two of them.

She hesitated. "You want the truth or a lie?"

His lips twitched. "The truth, the whole truth and nothing but the truth."

"The truth is you're a nice guy and a great kisser, but I have bigger fish to fry at the moment. If you're worried about me getting all clingy and having expectations or something…don't."

He sat back. "Brutal honesty. I like it." He ran a finger over his chin. "It *would* give me some breathing room. I have to be in Vancouver for meetings right after New Year's.…"

"There, you see?"

He frowned. "This all seems rather convenient."

She paused for a moment. Listened to the air blowing through the heater vents. Looked out at the street, awash in Christmas cheer.

"I don't want to be this person anymore," she whispered. "For years I've done exactly what my mother has done—accepted my lot in life and done a fair bit of complaining about it. It's not enough. Rhys said I was the last woman in the world he'd want to date. I don't want to be *the last woman in the world* for anything or anyone. I want to *do* something. I want to learn how. I would give anything to have the confidence and competence of someone like your sister. I've got to start somewhere. Please, Jack. I promise I'll do a good job for you. You won't regret it."

Jack stared at her, his eyes dark in the dim light of the car. He wasn't joking or smiling. Maybe that was what she liked about him. He didn't make fun of her, even when she made it easy for him.

"Can you be ready early on the twenty-sixth?"

"You set the time and I'll be waiting."

"And you've got a passport?"

"I do."

"Then you've got a deal. I'll call you with the details."

"Perfect." A smile broke out on her face. She was really going to do this. Something spontaneous, maybe even a little daring—at least in her small world. "You won't regret it, Jack," she repeated. "You'll see."

"I'm counting on it. Now get going. I've got to get back to the house and spend some time with the family." He held out his hand. "Should we shake on it?"

Amy peeled off her glove and put her hand in his. The moment their fingers touched sparks zinged up her arm and made her catch her breath. Her gaze rose to Jack's and she saw the same electricity reflected in his pupils.

"It won't get in the way," she assured him.

He pulled his hand away from hers. "Boxing Day morning. I'll pick you up on the way to the airport."

"See you then."

He didn't get out of the car this time, didn't go around to open her door or walk her to the steps. It was just as well. New boundaries had been set.

She hurried up the patio stones to the front door and turned just in time to see him pulling away from the curb.

He wouldn't regret it. She'd make sure.

Now she just had to break the news to her mother and pack her suitcase.

Chapter Three

Jack sincerely hoped he wasn't making a colossal mistake.

He looked over at Amy, who kept staring out the window of the Citation. He hadn't realized that she'd never flown before. When she'd said she had a passport, he'd assumed she'd traveled a little, but she remarked that she'd only had one for the odd trip across the border. When she'd discovered that he'd chartered a private plane for the trip, her usually big eyes got even bigger. And he'd thought she was about to swallow her tongue when he offered her breakfast once they were settled in the plush leather seats. It had only been coffee and croissants, but it didn't seem to matter to her. Everything was an adventure.

Her innocent surprise and pleasure made him feel about ten feet tall. Which was weird because he wasn't really into ego stroking. Maybe it was more that his life had gotten so busy that he tended to forget how special things were. He was worried about what was waiting for him in Montana. Amy was enjoying the journey.

Hmm. Maybe he needed to do a little more of that.

"What are you looking at?" he asked.

"Clouds. Isn't that amazing? We're above the clouds."

"And when we start our descent, you'll be able to see the ground. Mountains and everything."

"This is so cool. I never dreamed we were taking a private plane."

He chuckled and sat down beside her. "Hey, it's not like I own it." Though to be honest he'd considered it. He did enough traveling that it might be worth it. He could always lease it out to help cover the cost.

"Doesn't matter if it's yours or not," she said. "It's the coolest thing I've ever done."

Her smile was bright and contagious. She was going with him to help out, but he got the feeling that seeing her experience things for the first time was going to be fun. There were lots of things to do in and around the ranch. Maybe they could carve out some time for more than just work.

More than just work. The agreement was purely business, wasn't it?

He wanted to think so. Amy had asked him if he had a rescue complex and he'd denied it, but her question had hit rather close to home. Maybe he did. It had been years since Sheila and the following scandal, but it still left a bitter taste in his mouth. He'd tried to help. Tried to offer Sheila a way out. Rationally he knew it wasn't his fault she hadn't taken it. It didn't stop the guilt, though.

The truth was, he had stepped in at the wedding for two reasons. First, he'd seen the hurt on Amy's face. She'd looked first surprised at Rhys's put-down and then defeated, and he hated that. And then there was the fact that he was going crazy beneath the polite smiles and required happiness for Callum. Not that he begrudged his brother a thing. Avery was awesome and Callum's daughter, Nell, was sweet. But it was a stark reminder of what Jack might have had if things had been different, and Amy had been the perfect distraction.

He'd played it cool back in Cadence Creek. Slowed

things down the night of the wedding, hanging out with his parents instead of having a private toast for two in his room. Why, he couldn't say. He was pretty sure that if he'd pressed the issue, things might have ended in the morning rather than before midnight. But there was something innately sweet about Amy. She hadn't dug in her claws or tried to make the most of the situation.

And then there was the kiss. The one on the dance floor had whetted his appetite, a small amuse-bouche giving him a taste of what was to come. The kiss in the parlor of the B and B had been different. And still he'd shown restraint. Walked her home. Kissed her good-night at her door.

Then Christmas Eve had arrived and she'd been like a ray of sunshine in the midst of his stress. He'd convinced himself that they could just be friends. Especially when she came up with a very practical solution to his problem.

He frowned as he took another sip of coffee. They were going to be alone at Aspen Valley and now that they were on their way he was reminded of how very beautiful she was and how kissing her had left him wanting more. Much more.

Dammit. He was going to have to be careful, wasn't he? There was helping and then there was getting in way over his head....

They arrived at the small airport in Whitefish before lunch and transferred into his SUV that he'd left parked. It had snowed on Christmas Day and while the highways were fairly clear, the side roads were more snow-packed and he took his time. The sky was a clear, clear blue, the perfect backdrop for the mountains in the distance. When they finally turned onto the lane leading to his place, he heard Amy catch her breath.

"This is so beautiful. How far until we get to your ranch?"

He grinned, relaxing more and more as they got closer to home. "We're on it."

"All this is yours?"

He nodded, enchanted by the awe in her voice. "Most of it. It extends down past the valley there," he said, pointing. "We're bordered by a creek on the south side."

"How on earth do you look after it all? And run your company?"

He shrugged. "When I bought this place, I kept the foreman on staff, and most of the hands, too, to run the stock operation. They know way more about ranching than I do and so we all play to our strengths. I have a team in place to do the heavy lifting with Shepard Sports, so I can spend a lot of my time here." He grinned. "I couldn't give Callum a hard time about farming. I know exactly why he loves it. I'm enjoying the ranch far more than I expected."

Indeed he did. In the months after Sheila's betrayal and his devastating injury, he'd been lost. His heart had been trampled on and his dreams of Olympic gold ripped away. Even building Shepard Sports hadn't given him the fulfillment he'd expected. It was the ranch that had finally done it, where he felt like himself again.

"And the outdoor adventure part?" she asked.

"Satisfies my thrill quotient." He laughed a little. "The trail rides and cattle drives we do from here. For other events I either hire locally or partner with other businesses. It's good for the local economy."

"Things like the zip-lining? Are you still a daredevil, Jack?"

He shrugged. "Maybe, just a bit. I like the adrenaline rush, you know? There's that, and powder skiing, and rock climbing. There are other fun things, too, that are less hair-raising. You'll learn pretty quickly. Scheduling and confirming those activities are going to be on your to-do list this week."

She smiled back. "I feel like I'm in another world."

He turned his attention to the road. It was odd how her words so accurately reflected how he'd felt the first moment he'd arrived here, too. Like it was a world so completely detached from his crazy everyday life.

The lane widened at a break in the trees and there was the house, two and a half stories of wood siding stained a dark cherry, and a wraparound veranda surrounded by pristine white snowbanks.

Home.

The tension seeped out of his body as the car crawled up the drive and around the circular driveway to stop in front of the house. There was something about this place. Something that spoke to the deepest part of him. Whenever anything went wrong, when business was too crazy and the demands never-ending, a weekend here was all it took to center him again. When he needed solitude this was where he came. It was his hideaway. Sacred. Even when guests had free run of the house, it was okay. It was like he was offering them a glimpse of his corner of heaven. He didn't need to be greedy; he could share.

But to his recollection he'd never brought a woman here. Not that Amy was a woman in *that* sense. He just needed to keep telling himself that over the next several days.

He put the car in Park and shut off the ignition, then looked over at her.

"Holy crap," she whispered, staring at the lodge. "This place is huge." She turned to stare at him. "You own all this, *and* the apartment in Vancouver?"

He nodded. And he was on the cusp of buying another property, too, though that wasn't quite a done deal and he hadn't said a word about it to anyone but Callum. He'd had a meeting on the twenty-third, just before Christmas, and hopefully all that was left was to officially sign the papers and take possession once all the environmental inspections were completed.

"You really are rich, aren't you, Jack?"

He raised his eyebrows, surprised at the blunt question. "Was there ever any doubt?"

She shook her head. "Not really, not with how big Shepard Sports is. But you just...well...you don't act rich."

He knew it was a compliment. And it was something he made a point of—not letting success go to his head or change who he was. His jaw tightened a little, remembering how it felt to be on the receiving end of a man who wasn't afraid to throw his power and control around. Only then it hadn't been about money. It had been something entirely different. It had been about possession and dominance and it had altered Jack's life forever and in ways he hadn't expected.

Sheila had come to him and shown him the bruises. Jack had been so angry. So filled with rage. She was a lovely, gentle woman who deserved better. And this was at the hands of the man who was responsible for Jack's day-to-day training.

She'd convinced him to stay. That she needed him, and that he needed to train hard for the next Olympics. Their secret turned to more—to an affair—and Jack had been stuck firmly in the middle. He'd promised to find a new coach after the current season, to take her with him, keep her safe....

He'd let her down so badly. He frowned, pushing the

memory of his failures aside. "Let's get inside and get you settled, then I'll give you the grand tour. Tomorrow we can run into town and pick up some groceries and other necessities."

Together they got their bags out of the back and then Jack led the way up the steps and unlocked the door.

He watched as she crossed the threshold, put down her bag and gaped.

She was charming. There wasn't a pretentious, fake bone in her body. It was marvellous, seeing things through her eyes as she took them in for the first time. The past was the past, he reminded himself, and couldn't be changed. Maybe he'd lost the innocent, trusting part of himself but that didn't mean it didn't still exist in others.

His harsh introduction to reality had led him to the life he had now, and it was a good life. Sometimes he forgot how good, but he was reminded when he looked at Amy. She was enchanted, and by extension, he found her enchanting.

He found himself wishing they'd never struck the "no touch" bargain.

For better or worse, they were here. And for the next several days, he'd just have to keep temptation locked up. Amy had plans. Far be it from him to ruin them. This time he'd keep his promises. He wouldn't let her down.

SHE'D NEVER SEEN a house like this in her life.

Directly in front of her was a wide-open great room with soaring ceilings, an enormous stone fireplace and heavy wooden beams. Stairs climbed to another level and a railing overlooked the open foyer, bedecked in swooping evergreen boughs and red bows. A Christmas tree sat in the corner, a good twelve feet tall if she had her guess. The furniture was rugged, constructed of heavy wood and sturdy fabrics, and suited the grandeur of the house perfectly. To Amy, it felt like a cross between a log cabin and a rustic castle.

"Sorry about the lack of heat," Jack said from behind her. "Once I get the bags in, I'll get a fire going in the stove."

She spun around, still in awe of her surroundings. The fireplace faced the long sofa, but the huge flue also serviced a black iron stove on the opposite side. "You're not going to build one in the fireplace?"

He shrugged. "The woodstove throws better heat. The fireplace is better for atmosphere."

Clearly, he was siding with the practical here and away from having atmosphere with her. That was fine. Maybe in the evening she could light one and curl up with a book and a glass of wine....

Suddenly uncomfortable, she stepped farther inside so he could shut the door. It wasn't right that she was picturing such an indulgent scene when the deal was she was here to work. Not have Jack wait on her or lounge around drinking wine that he'd bought.

"What should I do first?" she asked.

He chuckled. "Wait here while I bring in your suitcase. I'll light a fire and take you on a tour of the house."

He was back in moments, deposited her case next to the door and shrugged off his jacket. "You want to hang these up while I get the wood?"

"Sure."

She hung up their coats and put her boots on a rubber mat then chafed her arms as she went farther inside the room. Jack kneeled in front of the heavy woodstove, adding little pieces of kindling until the fire caught. "There," he said, sitting back a bit. "Another minute or two and

I'll add some logs. Once it really gets going I'll turn the damper and before you know it we'll be toasty warm."

"Is wood your only source of heat?"

He shook his head. "Nope. The back of the house is south-facing and last year we put in solar panels. That's how we heat all our hot water, which also does our in-floor heating. Cool, right?"

She nodded and smiled at him. "Or hot, depending on how you look at it."

"There's something to be said for reducing our foot-print. I like the wood heat in the winter, though. I didn't have the heart to take it out. But little by little we've been making some sustainable changes."

"Oh?"

He stood up and brushed his hands on his jeans. "We expanded the vegetable garden, for example," he said. "Most of the vegetables we serve come from right here on the ranch. The beef certainly does. We buy locally for whatever we can—chicken, pork, out-of-season produce. Jeff and I—he's one of the hands—have talked about put-ting in a greenhouse, too. It would be awesome to have our own stuff during the winter."

"Are you turning into a farmer like your brother, Jack?"

He crossed his arms. "I don't know. Maybe. I love the sports thing and can't see giving it up entirely. But this is home. It makes me excited."

"You like to build things, face new challenges. You get bored easily, don't you?"

The smile slid from his face. "That's awfully percep-tive of you, considering you don't know me very well."

"Contrary to popular belief, I'm good at reading peo-ple."

He raised an eyebrow. "Oh? Give me an example."

Was he upset at her for her insight? It seemed clear as day to her. He'd competed at an international level in his sport. When that had ceased to be an option, he'd built himself a business empire. Once that was well on the way, he'd bought this place. She wondered what he'd do when he got bored with it. Or did his jumping around from thing to thing keep him from getting too close to people? She got the feeling that there was Work Jack and Private Jack and not many people got to see the private side.

He wanted proof that she could read people? She smiled. "Well, for example, at the wedding when I danced with Rhys. I knew he wasn't into me. What it looked like wasn't real at all. He only got close to me to make Taylor jealous. To make her see what she was missing. He only had eyes for her and I knew it."

"And it worked. They were arguing about you when he said what he did."

"Yeah."

He stepped closer. "You know, I think I'm pretty good at reading people, too. And you know what I think?"

He was only a few inches away from her. He wore a fleece pullover with a half zip that looked soft and cozy as anything. Even though the fire was beginning to throw some heat, she was still chilled. But starting to warm up a bit, simply having him so close to her. She had to tilt her chin to look up and meet his eyes. "What do you think?"

"I think you did it on purpose."

"Did what?" she asked, but her heart was beginning to pound.

"Set up Rhys and Taylor."

Their gazes clashed for a few seconds more before she dropped her gaze. "That would be stupid, wouldn't it? Considering how it ended for me. Looking like an idiot."

He put a finger under her chin and lifted it. "Maybe

you felt so foolish because you'd been trying to help and got stomped on for it. It would really burn my biscuits if I did something noble like that and was then told how undesirable I was."

It had burned her biscuits, too, and she let out a long breath. "I knew she liked him. I saw them together when she first arrived in town. They had dinner at the diner. And then at Avery's shower, his name came up and she blushed. We made fun of her that night, just a little. But it was clear there was something going on. At the wedding they were avoiding each other. I just wanted to give them a little nudge."

"It worked."

She smiled weakly. It had worked, all right. All a person had to do was be in the same room with Rhys and Taylor and they could feel the sparks.

"You're smarter than you let on, aren't you?"

She held his gaze. "You figured that out pretty fast."

"I'm good at reading people, too. And my guess is people see you a certain way and don't bother to look too deeply beneath the surface."

"Right again. Which is why I'm ready to break away. Do something new. In a way, I kind of have to thank Rhys. What he said kind of jolted me out of my rut."

"Yay for Rhys."

They were so close together now her thick sweater brushed lightly against his pullover. The touch was so light it shouldn't have had any effect on her whatsoever, but it did. Being so near Jack raised her heart rate and her temperature. It wasn't that he was rolling in money. Had little to do with who he was or even his looks. It was that for the first time in her life, she was standing face-to-face with a man who didn't see her with a warning label plastered across her forehead. He understood her without even having to try very hard. Forget what Rhys had done—it was Jack who'd convinced her to face things head-on. He'd been the one to nudge her into taking action.

While they were standing there, his gaze slid away from her eyes to settle at her lips as they drifted closer, closer together...

Amy stepped back. She was already feeling slightly over her head with Jack. To explore something physical would be just about the stupidest thing she could do. Maybe he understood her but the reality was that his life and hers were drastically different. This would end up going nowhere, and if she allowed herself to get too close she'd only get hurt in the end. She was here to give Jack a hand and to get away and enjoy the scenery.

Jack couldn't be included in that scenery. It would only complicate her plans.

She cleared her throat. "Why don't you take me on that tour now," she suggested. "And then show me the office so I can get started."

"If that's what you want."

His voice was low and suggested he'd rather be doing something else. It was so, so tempting.

But a little voice inside her said that having a fling with Jack was exactly what everyone would expect her to do. If she wanted people to expect better from her, she should start expecting better from herself.

She squared her shoulders. "Yes, I think it is."

His eyes were far too knowing, but he stepped back rather than press his case and she let out the breath she'd been holding.

"Come on, then," he said. "We'll start with the downstairs. The kitchen's right through here."

He turned away and Amy followed after him. She

stared at his back—at his broad shoulders, his lean hips and the perfect way he filled out a pair of jeans. She had to be crazy to turn that down. Crazy, and stupid for thinking this was ever a good idea to begin with.

Chapter Four

Amy made one final notation on the calendar before shutting the program down and taking a breath. Rosa—Jack's regular manager—ran a tight ship. Once Amy had the passwords, it had been easy as anything to access the schedule, contact list and even Rosa's weekly to-do list, which was a finely tuned document.

The problem was that the to-do list was several days behind, so Amy had spent the past two hours familiarizing herself with the setup and then attending to the first items on the list—the most urgent being booking confirmations and writing checks for invoices that needed immediate payment. Tomorrow would be time enough to get a really good look at the accounting setup so she could enter income and expenses without messing up Rosa's system. Right now she had brain overload. Considering there were ten people arriving in less than three days, she had a lot to learn. She hadn't even touched on what her duties would be once they got here.

A knock interrupted her thoughts and she looked up to find Jack standing in the doorway, his brows furrowed. "Is something wrong?" she asked. She took off her reading glasses and put them on top of the desk.

"I didn't know you wore glasses."

"Just reading ones for close-up. Not usually an issue,

but this afternoon turned out to be a little intense on the eyes."

"You should have taken a break a few hours ago."

"A few hours?" She stared up at him as he crossed the room to the desk. "What time is it?"

"After seven."

She slumped in the chair. "No wonder my eyes were starting to cross." She laughed a little. "I guess I lost track of time."

"No kidding. I got caught up in work, too, and then started dinner when the stomach started rumbling. Are you hungry?"

She hadn't been, or at least hadn't taken the time to think about it. But now she realized her tummy did feel a little hollow. They'd had some canned soup around two o'clock but it had been a light meal and that was hours ago. "You cooked?"

"Of course I did. When I'm here Rosa does a lot of the cooking, but it's not like I have a personal chef all the time. There wasn't much in the way of fresh produce, but I roasted a chicken, made a risotto from a package and found a bag of frozen broccoli."

It was starting to make absolutely no sense that the guy was single. And she might have said something to that effect except her stomach growled in the silence and she clapped a hand over her abdomen.

"Sold," she said drily. "But can you sign these checks first? A couple are a few days overdue and since I don't have signing authority…"

"Of course." He came around the desk and grabbed a pen.

"I've got the envelopes ready. I can mail them tomorrow if we go into town."

"Sounds perfect." He leaned over the desk and for a

few minutes the only sound was the scratch of the pen on paper. Amy took the few moments to let her gaze travel over him. Faded jeans shouldn't look so good on a man, and the fleece pullover only helped to make his shoulders appear broader and his hips leaner. His hair, a bit lighter than his brother's, was just long enough that a girl could run her hands through it and tease the slight curls on the ends. She swallowed. She could handle this, right? It was just an itty-bitty attraction. She just had to remind herself of the facts and keep her head out of the clouds.

And she would have done just that except he finished signing the checks, stood up tall and held out the pen. "There. That'll keep the wolf from the door for another few weeks."

As if he had to worry about it. She was far more concerned with the wolf standing before her. His easy good looks didn't fool her one bit. Jack Shepard was a man who found what he wanted and was used to getting it. The fact that he managed to do so while being absolutely charming only made him more dangerous.

"Great. Thanks. I'm starving." *Awesome response,* she thought, nearly rolling her eyes at her own awkwardness.

To her relief he moved off, giving her room to get up from the desk and follow him out of Rosa's office. Once she hit the hallway she caught the first scents of dinner. Jack led her back to the kitchen, where he'd set the small table for their meal, the small hanging light fixture providing a cozy, intimate glow. She was glad he'd chosen to eat in this room. The dining room was too big with its table for twelve.

"I can't believe you made dinner," she said, even more off balance when he politely pulled out her chair for her to sit down.

"You seemed pretty involved in work when I went past

the door earlier. I figured it was the least I could do. And it's nothing fancy."

"Still, you said it was Rosa's job…"

"But I never said it was yours." He put a few bowls on the table and then picked up a carving knife and began slicing the chicken. "Don't get me wrong, you've got free rein of the kitchen while you're here, and we can share cooking duties when it's the two of us if you like. But I don't expect you to cook for guests, Amy. Not when you're not used to it. This afternoon I hired someone to come out during our bookings and look after the meals. The only thing you might have to do is purchase the groceries from our suppliers."

He took his seat, smiled and handed her the platter. "Dig in."

Amy served herself the chicken, risotto and vegetables and took a tentative bite. It was simple but delicious, and as they ate Jack answered many of Amy's questions about the ranch and the retreat business. In particular she was nervous about doing the accounting, since she was unfamiliar with U.S. tax laws and reporting practices.

"Don't worry about that," Jack reassured her. "If you can keep up with what comes in and what goes out, we'll be fine for now. Once Rosa's a bit better, I can take the laptop to her place and help her relieve some boredom while she's laid up. She'll go crazy after a few weeks, guaranteed. Worst-case scenario is I bring in someone from my accounting department at head office to help out."

Amy had answered emails and looked after little details, but now she was starting to wonder if Jack actually had enough work to keep her busy for the next few weeks. Once she was caught up, it would be a breeze, wouldn't it? Especially if he'd hired someone to help out….

It made her feel a little like she was taking advantage of the situation. Using him.

Jack pushed his plate away and gave a satisfied sigh. "There, that filled the hole." He leaned back in his chair. "How are you set for tomorrow? Do you think you're going to be chained to your desk?"

"I've got your next week caught up as far as bookings and events, but I was planning on getting a good look at your accounting program so I can enter in the invoices you just paid. And I'm assuming the payment when the group arrives on the twenty-eighth will need to be processed. The balance is still due, right?"

"That's right."

"And then there's going into town for groceries, and to the post office."

His lips twitched a little. "I never took you for the 'all work and no play' type."

She put down her fork. "I don't view this trip as a free ride, Jack. I'm here to earn my keep."

"Still, you could steal a few hours."

Her heart did a strange little patter. He wanted to steal her away? For what? The idea of playing hooky with the boss was pretty intriguing, but it wasn't why she was here. "I probably shouldn't."

"What if your boss orders it?"

She met his gaze. His eyes were full of impish humor. What on earth was she doing? She felt completely out of her depth. Jack was older, more experienced certainly, worldly. She'd barely been outside Cadence Creek, had only ever had one serious relationship. Had she really thought she could come all the way down here and stay in his house and stay completely immune?

She didn't know how to act. Some women could handle this sort of situation with grace and confidence but she wasn't one of them. "What did you have in mind?"

"It's a surprise," he answered.

That didn't make her feel any better.

"I promise you'll have fun," he added, smiling a little.

"Jack, I…"

"What?"

She floundered, trying to put words together to express what she desperately needed him to understand. What would surprise everyone back in Cadence Creek if they knew the truth. That other than her relationship at age nineteen, she hadn't slept with a man. Not even Sam Diamond.

Maybe she'd dated—a lot. But that didn't mean she slept around. And perhaps that was why it hurt so much. People made assumptions without caring about the person inside. If it weren't for her mom she would have left Cadence Creek in her dust long ago. But her mom had already been abandoned once. Amy didn't have it in her to let it happen again.

"I'm not very good at this. I think…I might need some clarification about exactly what you…um…expect."

His gaze warmed as he understood her meaning. "You mean about us?"

God, this was embarrassing. How presumptuous to think he'd expect anything in the romantic—no, scratch that—the sexual way. A man like him and a woman like her. But then she remembered the way he'd kissed her in the bed-and-breakfast living room and the way he'd looked at her while they were dancing and the hope she kept trying to tamp down threatened to flutter loose on little butterfly wings.

Besides, she had to know. She didn't want it to be this awkward for the rest of the trip.

"Yes," she answered quietly. "With us."

He was quiet for a long moment. A moment during which her cheeks heated and her body felt like it was shrinking back into her chair. This was why things never worked out. She had no clue what she was doing when it came to men.... She misread signals, came on too strong, too clingy....

"What I expect is whatever you're comfortable with," he finally answered. "You came here to help me out in a pinch. I could lie to you and say this is strictly business. Is that what you want?"

She swallowed, hard. He could say it but it would hold no power because he'd already admitted he'd be lying. He leaned forward a little so that the space between them at the table got smaller. Heck, the whole room felt smaller.

"I don't think so."

But she couldn't look at him.

He got up from the table and her breath caught for a bit—she was unsure of what he was doing. But he went to the fridge and took out a box. She watched, fascinated, as he cut two pieces of dessert and put them on plates, and then came back to the table. He put one plate in front of her. When she looked up at him, his eyes were smiling. "You look like you could use some chocolate," he said.

"You've no idea," she replied.

He chuckled a little, just a warm tease of a laugh as he pulled his chair closer and put his own plate beside hers. "You keep surprising me," he admitted, picking up his fork. "I have this idea of who you are and then it keeps changing."

"Right back atcha," she said. "I think you might be a little more complicated than you try to appear."

Again with the charming smile. "Why would you say that?"

"Nobody can possibly be this nice, this perfect."

The smile faded. "Believe me, I'm far from perfect."

He put some cheesecake on his fork and held it out. He was feeding her now? More like changing the subject—something she realized he was quite good at. Her stomach swirled with nerves as silence settled around them. Tentatively she leaned forward and closed her lips around the fork.

He pulled the fork away, leaving her with the creamy chocolate bite on her tongue. It was heavenly, and she closed her eyes for a second and let the flavors mingle. Dark chocolate, cream cheese, salted caramel. "That is seriously delicious," she murmured.

When she opened her eyes, Jack was watching her, his expression hungry. Self-conscious now, she picked up her fork and slid it into her piece of cake and then popped it in her mouth. If he was expecting her to return the favor…feeding him was too intimate. Too suggestive. Which might be okay at another time, but not when she was so unsure. Not when it felt like they were standing on quicksand and one wrong move would make the earth shift beneath them. And definitely not when there was no escape route or another soul around to run interference.

He didn't say anything at first, just scooped up some of his own rich dessert. It was nearly half-gone when he spoke again.

"So are we just going to dance around this attraction for your entire visit?"

He asked it so casually that she did a double take, replaying the words in her head.

"I've never done this before," she admitted. "I told you back in Cadence Creek that this was different, out of my comfort zone."

"Amy," he said quietly, and he reached out and tucked

a piece of hair behind her ear. "Can you possibly be as innocent as you seem?"

She didn't know how to react, whether she should pull away, or answer with a smart remark, or be honest. So she froze beneath the gentle touch, on the precipice of giving in and leaning closer.

"I'm not..." Her face flamed. "I'm not feeling like I'm on equal ground here, okay? And I didn't come here to have a fling with you."

He smiled, that slow, devastating smile. "I believe you. You're far too skittish to be practiced at this."

"I'm not sure if that's a compliment or not." She got up from the table and went to the sink, put her plate in the bottom and tried to steady her breathing. It had been far easier dealing with emails and invoices than the seductive reality of Jack.

He got up and followed her. "It's a surprise. In Cadence Creek you were different." He smiled a little. "Sassy. More sure of yourself, in control."

"I was in my element."

"And it was easy because that's the Amy people expect, right? Where did she go?"

She was a little stunned at his quick insight. He was right. There was Cadence Creek Amy, who hid behind bright smiles and bouncy curls and a "shrug it off" attitude, and there was the woman standing here. And this woman was feeling a bit naked, stripped of her regular armor.

"What do you want me to say?"

He shook his head, put his plate on the counter just behind her and put his hands into his pockets. Even so, he was standing remarkably close, so close she could smell the scent of his cologne. It was Jack who was in his element here. He was his own man…and that man was impressive.

"How about the truth? I usually find it's a good place to start."

He was far too close now, and all her senses were clamoring. "I think I might be a little out of my depth, Jack."

He gave a little nod, as if considering her words. "With the job or with me?"

Oh, dear Lord, he was making it difficult. Her pulse was pounding against her wrist and it was hard to think straight with his gaze so intent on her. "I can do the job no trouble," she answered, hating that she sounded a little breathless.

"So it's me."

"Look at you," she responded. "Elite athlete. Businessman. Millionaire. Do you blame me for feeling a little intimidated?"

He frowned then. "That's what I am. Not who."

The words struck her with their honesty, a brief moment of insight that she'd been right—there was more beneath the surface than outward appearance. Perhaps Jack was as tired of the labels forced on him as she was of hers. "I'm sorry," she said quietly. "But I can't help it. I look around myself here, in this place, with you, and think I've landed in an alternate reality."

"And it scares you?"

She looked away. "A little bit, yeah."

"Because…"

"Because I don't fit in here. Because I'm a round peg in a square hole. Because I'm…afraid I'll embarrass myself. Embarrass you."

"I know," he said quietly.

"You do?"

"I'm not blind," he answered. "You're in a new place, with new things, and with me, who is pretty much a stranger. I mean I'm not really, but I'm not someone you've known your whole life, either. Your safety net has been taken away. And you know what? When you stop being scared of it being gone, you'll be glad. It'll be the best thing to happen to you. You wait and see."

"That's a bit presumptuous of you. You hardly know me. And it sounds…" She struggled to find the right word. "Smug."

He shrugged. "Not at all. I see it all the time in the Aspen Valley clients. Besides, it wasn't that long ago that I was you. I lost my safety net. It was why I bought this place. It changed me."

"You lost your safety net?"

"Sure I did. When I couldn't ski anymore."

"But you said that an athlete was what you were, not who."

Consternation showed on his face. Had he expected her to let him off, especially after he'd managed to pry into her life? Not a chance.

"So I did. But that doesn't account for what it meant to me. No matter what was going on in my life, I could always count on a time when it was just me and the hill. Nothing else. And then suddenly I had nowhere to put all the pent-up energy and anger and…and stuff. I didn't know who I was. Until I came here and it all came together."

He paused, then came so close that they were hardly a breath apart. "Let go of your safety net and be yourself, Amy. No one will ask you to be anything more. Or anything less."

His hands found hers, and linked together, they rested against the edge of the countertop. Slowly, gently, he touched his lips to hers. The kiss was soft, undemanding, and took her apart bit by bit, peeling away the layers of her reservations one by one until she melted against him.

Jack pulled away by degrees, a gradual sliding away until their lips parted with a sad sigh of goodbye. Amy ran her tongue over hers, tasting him there.

"You are a beautiful woman," he murmured. "I'd be crazy not to want to be with you. But nothing more, unless you want it. You got it? You call the shots. I won't be accused of taking advantage."

She blinked, trying to clear the haze in her head that was simply filled with Jack. "You're not… We're not…"

"Not tonight," he answered easily. "Not ever, if you're not ready. I would never force a woman to do anything she didn't want."

"You're talking about wanting to sleep with me," she stated, wishing she could take back the incredulous tone in her voice. It made her sound terribly naive and guileless.

His lips curved up, just a little bit. "Don't sound so surprised. You're a desirable woman."

No one had ever come right out and said that to her before. She'd rather die than admit that those simple words touched emotions deep inside her. That they meant more to her than he'd ever understand.

"There are no expectations, Amy." He ran his thumb across her cheek. "No…context. Just you and me."

He was so devastatingly sexy and patient she was sure he was using some reverse psychology trick on her, because she was very, very close to wrapping herself around him and saying to hell with the consequences. But something about him made her step back. Maybe it was the look on his face when he spoke about losing his safety net. Maybe there was the niggling sense at the back of her mind that for all his confidence and successful exterior, there was something vulnerable about Jack. A soft spot that he guarded well. There was more to it than losing his ski career. More than a busted knee.

He kissed her forehead then. "It's only for a few weeks. I don't want you to do anything you might regret later. Be sure."

Right. Finally, common sense intruded on the heels of his last words. It was only for a few weeks. This thing with Jack was simple chemistry. There was no room for fantasies or getting carried away.

There was letting go of the safety net and then there was BASE jumping headfirst off a cliff. And while she totally looked at this time as a way of breaking free of her routine, of using it as an experiment, she was still too cautious to play daredevil with her heart—especially with a man who came right out and said he was temporary. That so wasn't the fairy tale she had in mind.

"Thanks, Jack," she murmured, sliding out from between his body and the cupboard. "I'm a bit tired. I thought I'd call my mom and then make an early night of it. I'll see you in the morning?"

"Good night."

Halfway up the stairs she felt slightly guilty about leaving him with the dishes, but she'd had to get out of there before she threw all her good sense out the window and ignored all the warning bells.

And when the sound of dishes clanking in the sink echoed up the stairs to her open door, she shut it and ran a hot bath.

Chapter Five

Despite lying awake until half past one, Jack was up early the next morning and out at the barns, catching up with Miguel and Raffy. Miguel was his main horseman, while Raffy looked after the cattle operation, but the two of them worked together more often than not, a real Mutt-and-Jeff routine that kept the rest of the hands in good spirits. This time of year required fewer staff, so when Jack strolled through the horse barn, his boots echoing on the concrete, he could hear the sounds of a recent country hit on the barn radio and the wheezy sound of Raffy's laughter as Miguel told him some story. Jack was relieved to hear the laughter. Miguel was also Rosa's husband, and the family had been through a lot since the accident.

"Boys," he greeted, turning the corner into the barn office.

Two coffee mugs sat on the table, steam rolling off, and a paper bag with muffins. "Get you a cup, boss?"

"That'd be great," he said, pulling up a stool to the table. "Whose muffins? Bet you're missing Rosa's baking, Miguel."

"I can live with store-bought muffins for a few weeks, I guess," he answered quickly, and Jack saw the strain around the man's eyes.

"You been sleeping okay, amigo?" Jack accepted the cup of black coffee and snagged a muffin.

"Naw, not so much. It'll be better when Rosa is home from the hospital."

"You need help with anything? Getting her room set up, wheelchair, that sort of thing?"

"You've already done more than enough, Jack," Miguel said, staring into his cup. "I don't know how to thank you."

Jack put down his cup. "You're family. That's all there is to it. If you need anything, you say the word. Got it?"

"Yes, sir."

Raffy—short for Raphael—nodded. "That goes for me and Isabel, too. Izzy's gonna fix you up with some freezable meals and stuff."

"Worst part is gonna be keeping that woman occupied," Miguel lamented. "She ain't used to sittin' much and she's awful worried about how you're gonna keep things going here."

"You tell her not to worry. I brought in some temporary help. A friend of my brother's from Canada. But it's just temporary, mind. You make sure she knows her job is safe."

A friend of his brother's seemed the easiest way to explain his relationship to Amy, but Jack knew it wasn't true at all. On Christmas Eve he'd been trying to come up with a way to spend more time with her—he enjoyed her company—and she'd conveniently offered to help him out, saving him the trouble of coming up with a proposition.

Her behavior at dinner last night had been a surprise, though. The dynamic, bubbly Amy Wilson was a bit of a front after all. He'd caught glimpses of different sides of her yesterday. A capable, intelligent and efficient side as she took over Rosa's desk and tackled the work with barely a batted eyelid. And a softer, far more innocent side last night as she let down her guard.

He understood far better than she knew. After all, he'd built a shell around himself after Sheila left him. It was easier to let people think he was a bit of a playboy, easier to hide behind the facade of a sharp businessman, than to let the painful reality show.

The blown knee had been nothing. Nothing compared to the way Sheila had broken his heart. He'd put it all on the line for her, and she'd stood by while Chase—her husband and Jack's coach—had used his fists to get his point across.

"Man or woman?" Raffy asked, pulling him out of his thoughts. It took him a second to realize Raffy was asking about Amy.

"Woman, and she's a looker, so keep your wandering eye in check or I'll have a word with your wife." Jack let a grin crawl up his cheek. Miguel was close to fifty and he suspected that Raffy was a little older than that. Both had kids that were grown and moved away. Still, they knew how to turn on the charm.

"Friend of your brother's, my eye," Raffy said shrewdly. "First time you've brought a girl here, though. Is it serious?"

"It's not like that. She's a temp. She's going to be studying hospitality management next year. It's a good gig for her for a few weeks." Even as he said it he knew he was being a big fat liar. There was definitely more going on, whether they ever acted on it or not.

Miguel's face fell. "Rosa's going to be out a few months, boss."

"I know, buddy. I know. It's fine. When Amy goes home, I'll make other arrangements. It was too hard to get someone else on short notice, especially at Christmas. And I was thinking…when Rosa's up to it, we can set her up with a laptop at home for some light work. Answering email, that sort of thing. It might keep both of you from killing each other."

"I think she'd like that. For now…" Miguel's voice fell off. "She's in a lot of pain."

Jack put his hand on his friend's arm. Miguel had been the first person Jack had kept on when he'd bought the ranch. It had been Miguel who'd taught him the ropes with the horses, had taken him on his first trail rides. Who'd sat around a campfire at night and said nothing at all—just let Jack be Jack. He'd do anything for this man who was like a second father.

"You need some time off, chief?"

"No, sir."

"If you ever do, you'd better tell me. We'll manage."

"That's right," Raffy agreed. "Speaking of, I've got a herd to move today. Stacks are nearly gone in that east pasture. Gonna move them one over today."

"I should finish up, too. It's nice today. Thought I'd put the horses out in the south corral, let them soak in some sun, enjoy the free space. Farrier's coming to look at Gem's hoof crack, too."

"I'm going into town in a few hours. You need anything, make a list and bring it on up to the house."

"You got it."

Raffy shrugged on his jacket and pulled a pair of worn gloves from the pocket. "Catch you fellas later."

After he was gone, Jack stood up. "You need some help this morning?"

"Nope. Got it all under control."

Jack nodded. "That's good."

"Good to see you back here, Jack. You always show

up looking tired and leave looking ten years younger," Miguel said.

"Don't I know it." Jack grinned. "Must be the good company."

"It's the wide-open space and the horses, and you know it. You gonna get this girl out on horseback while she's here? Pretty little view from the crest above the creek. But then you know that…."

"You doing a little matchmaking, chief?"

Miguel's rusty laugh rang through the room. "I know better than to try that. But I'm gonna enjoy watching you tumble when you meet the right woman. It's gonna be right humbling for you, son."

"Go on," Jack replied, laughing. "I'll see you later."

"You bet."

Jack whistled on his way out of the barn and back to the house. Not in a million years had he ever considered himself a rancher. And he had a lot to learn. But one thing he'd come to realize for sure—it was in his blood. Maybe he lacked knowledge and experience, but those would come in time. When it came down to brass tacks, he'd rather have a pair of dirty boots and a golden sunset over the Montana hills than a skyline from a boardroom window anytime.

When he opened the front door, he heard a string of cursing coming from the kitchen. His grin grew, blossoming into laughter as he caught the edges of a conversation Amy was apparently having with one of his appliances. He took off his boots and walked in his stocking feet to the kitchen.

"Okay, you hunk of junk. The blue light is on so *you're* on. Now I'm going to press this button and so help me God you're going to work or I'm gonna kick you in the…"

"Good morning," he said.

She spun around, a hand pressed to her chest in surprise as her cheeks blossomed an adorable pink. "Um... good morning?"

He laughed, something he found himself doing around her more than he normally did.

"I'm working on the assumption that it's not a good morning until you've had your first cup of coffee," he suggested.

"That's a good assumption." She frowned. "I can't figure out your stupid machine." She muttered something unladylike under her breath.

Jack liked the look of the "new" Amy before him. Sure, he'd found her incredibly beautiful each time they'd met. And each time she'd been dressed nicely, her hair styled and makeup perfectly applied. But this morning she had her curls bunched in a matted ponytail, her face was devoid of any cosmetics and she wore white pajama pants covered with tiny images of Mickey Mouse and a white T-shirt.

He fought the urge to go up and cuddle her close, kiss her good-morning and tease away the caffeine-deprived grumpiness.

He went forward, calmly inserted a coffee packet, clicked the lid shut and pressed a button.

"That's it?"

"That's it. Of course, you can always froth milk over here...." He gestured toward an attachment. "But you might want to start simply first."

"We just have a regular old coffee machine at my mom's," she explained. "You know, paper filter, coffee grounds, pour water in the top..."

"We have that here, too, for when we want coffee for the masses." The first cup finished brewing. "Do you take milk?" he asked.

She shook her head. "Not today. There isn't any."

"Oh. Right."

She wiggled her fingers. "It's okay. I'll survive."

But Jack shook his head. "Get another cup. I have a better idea."

This time he inserted a cappuccino-flavored packet in the machine. Before long the liquid sputtered through and the scent of coffee and vanilla wafted through the kitchen. "Try this," he said, handing it to her.

"Oh, that's good," she said, closing her eyes after the first sip. "I almost feel human."

"Breakfast?"

She shrugged. "No milk, no bread, no eggs."

"Looks like I'm taking you out, then."

"I'm not much of a breakfast eater. It's okay."

"I am," he answered definitively. "Besides, I've been up and visiting the guys in the barn already. Why don't you go have a quick shower. The sooner we go, the sooner we can get back."

"The guys in the barn?"

"You didn't expect the animals to look after themselves, did you?"

Her blue eyes seemed extra wide. "I guess I didn't think about there being anyone but us here."

"Miguel is Rosa's husband, and Raffy lives with his wife just this side of town. They kind of came with the ranch." He smiled at her and sipped at his coffee, very aware that this was his second cup on an empty stomach. He'd better be careful or he'd be wired. He put the cup down and leaned back against the counter. "I knew next to nothing about ranching when I bought the place. Everything I know I've learned from the two of them. In a few months Raffy will look like the walking dead when calving season begins. We've only got a small herd, but it's enough to keep us busy, and our big spring event is in late May or early June, when we do the branding and then a short cattle drive to where they'll graze the summer, including overnight camping. There's not much peace and quiet that week, but it's kind of magical, too."

"Sounds dirty," she commented.

He kept forgetting she wasn't a farm girl. Though why he expected her to be, he wasn't sure. It wasn't like he was the poster boy for Western life or anything.

"Dirt washes," he replied, but he felt a little let down that she didn't share his enthusiasm. He wasn't sure why. Amy was temporary, just the way he liked it. Nothing too serious. Nothing too deep.

"Speaking of, I'd better take that shower if we're going out," she suggested. "And check the email. I'm waiting for the chef you hired to send me a shopping list. Ten people plus you and me for four days, right?"

"Sounds about right. Then we've got a few days off before a smaller group comes in for the weekend."

She was back to all business again. Jack knew he should be relieved, so why was he annoyed at her persistence to keep things so straightforward? He thought he'd broken through a bit last night when they'd kissed. Not that he was going to force the issue, but even so. She didn't need to be nervous. He wasn't going to hurt her, after all.

She was so very determined to do things right that he got the feeling she was not going to have any fun at all. And that wasn't the idea behind bringing her down here. It was possible to do both. He'd learned how. The least he could do was pass along the favor.

The drive into town was gorgeous. Amy kept staring out the window at the tall evergreens blanketed with snow.

The sky was crisply blue and the air as clear as glass and just about as sharp, sitting at just a few degrees above freezing. She was used to the cold, after all, and this was the perfect winter's day.

Jack sat beside her, his eyes focused straight on the winding road, but his hands relaxed on the wheel. He'd been 100 percent sexy this morning, hadn't he? His cheeks wind-kissed from the cold, smelling like the outdoors and dressed all manly and stuff in his jeans and flannel shirt. So different from the guy in the tux she remembered. That guy had been smooth and in charge. This Jack was just as in charge as ever, but there were rougher edges about him out here. What surprised her most was that she liked him this way.

She wasn't sure how she was going to get through the next few weeks. Last night she'd fallen completely under his spell as he'd kissed her. That couldn't happen again. She wasn't going to fall back into old patterns—that would just mess everything up. She had to keep focused on the big picture and not get distracted.

Jack pulled into a parking spot a few doors down from a café that reminded Amy a lot of the Wagon Wheel, the diner in Cadence Creek. He held the door for her and once they were inside she realized she was starving. The smells of bacon and toast and fresh coffee were nearly too much. Jack's hand rested lightly on the hollow of her back as he guided her to a table for two along the big front window. "You're going to love it here," he said, waiting until she was seated to take his own chair. "Don't you dare repeat this, but I think the omelets here are better than Martha Bullock's."

Amy smiled. "That's a bold statement. At least you didn't challenge her pie. That might have caused an international incident."

The lopsided grin graced his face again and she went warm all over.

A waitress came over with menus and a pot of coffee…the real stuff, not the milky cappuccino-flavored stuff that Amy had sipped this morning. It had satisfied her immediate need but now she needed the full brew.

"Well, Jack Shepard. Good to see you back."

"Hi, Marianne." Jack looked up at the waitress. "How's Junior?"

"Growing like a bad weed. Got his first tooth a few weeks ago."

"Before you know it he'll be out snowboarding with his dad."

"Don't even." She smiled and filled their coffee cups.

"This is Amy Wilson. She's helping us out for a few weeks while Rosa's in the hospital."

Marianne was gracious and offered a warm smile. "Nice to meet you. Jack's got quite an operation going out at Aspen Valley. Really turned that place around when he bought it."

Amy wondered what she meant by "turning it around," but merely smiled. "It's in a beautiful spot. I just got here yesterday, so I'm still learning the ropes."

"We'd better get you fueled up, then." She rattled off the breakfast specials. Amy knew she should keep to fruit and oatmeal, but she couldn't resist the idea of pancakes with scrambled eggs and bacon. She'd just call this brunch and not eat again later….

When Marianne was gone, Amy looked at Jack. "Okay, so this place might be more resortish, but it's looking a lot like Cadence Creek from where I'm sitting."

Jack added sugar and cream to his coffee, something she realized he hadn't done this morning. "Is that a problem?" he asked.

She shrugged. "Not really, I guess."

"There's a core population of locals, but it's mostly tourists."

"And yet…everyone knows everyone else, right?"

"I suppose." He put down his spoon. "You prefer more anonymity."

"Of course. It's exactly what I don't like about home. Everyone sticking their noses in my business."

"But no one knows you here. You don't have, I don't know, context."

She shrugged. It wasn't just that; it was trading one place she didn't like for an identical one. It was okay that he didn't really get it. He didn't need to. "No worries, Jack. You like it here and that's all that matters. You're the one who lives here."

"Maybe I was hoping you'd like it here, too."

She took a drink of coffee. It was hot and rich, just the way she liked it. "Why should it matter?"

His face flattened and he looked out the window. There was a slight pause before he answered. "I guess if you're going to spend a few weeks here, it might be nice if you enjoyed yourself, too, that's all."

"I'm here to work."

"Dammit, I know that."

She sat back a bit. "Why are you so snappy all of a sudden?"

Marianne came back with their plates and saved Jack from answering right away. Once she was gone he added salt and pepper to his eggs and then offered her the shakers.

She took them, her stomach turning nervously. This was supposed to be simple. Her helping him, getting away for a few weeks. No funny business. But it was a mess. First with the kiss last night, and then with the fact that she couldn't stop thinking about him. And knowing deep down that she wanted this time in her life to be different. She wanted to prove to herself that for once she wasn't chasing some guy. That she could see a bigger picture.

That she'd grown up.

Except Jack wasn't making it easy at all. And she didn't want to admit that she was a little bit scared or that she was worried about what would happen to her mother if she were left all alone. Would she withdraw further into her shell? Maybe Amy could spend some time over the next few months really trying to get Mary out more. Involved in something....

"I'm sorry I was short with you," he said quietly.

"Maybe this wasn't such a great idea," she replied, her appetite waning. Still, she diligently drizzled syrup onto her pancakes and cut into them with automatic motions.

"You don't want to stay?" His gaze snapped up to hers.

"Relax. I wouldn't leave you in the lurch like that. And it's not that I want to go. It's that..." She put down her fork, the bite untasted. "It's just that this isn't as simple as I made it out to be. You're confusing things." She gave him a wry smile. "It would be much easier if you were, I don't know, fifty, with grey hair and a potbelly."

His gaze tethered her. "There's this *thing,* right?"

"Right. But... Oh, hell. It's complicated. This *thing,* as you call it, is not why I came here."

"I know that. You wanted to get away. To get out from under the microscope. To see something different." He frowned. "Is that it? It's not different?"

She forced herself to think before answering, so she picked up a strip of bacon and took a bite. She didn't reply until she'd swallowed and had a chance to consider what she was going to say. How much to tell him. How transparent she wanted to be.

"We're at breakfast on my first full day. People know you. And I can't help but wonder if the fact that I'm here with you is a topic of conversation."

"Who cares?"

She sighed. "I don't want to be *that girl,* Jack. That I got hired because you and I are…whatever it is we aren't."

"You care far too much about what other people think about you. What does it matter? All that matters is what you think about yourself."

"Easy for you to say. Do you know that when I went into the bathroom at the wedding, the women laughed when they realized who I was? As if it were expected. I could picture the eye rolls. All because Cadence Creek is so small that mistakes are made in full view of the population."

Jack speared a piece of egg. "Take that bathroom and multiply it by a thousand. A million. Try finding your romantic failures splashed over international papers."

Fast on and off the hill. "That was years ago. Do people really remember?"

He shrugged and kept methodically eating his meal. "Some do. A lot did in the first few years after it happened. If I wasn't known as the guy who'd crashed his Olympic dreams away, I was the guy who'd had an affair with his coach's wife." His face looked sour. "My point is, it wasn't easy for me. I've been there. And in the end it doesn't pay to give a good damn what other people think."

If he weren't careful, he was going to stab right through the plate rather than into his slice of ham. Was his charming exterior his way of showing he didn't care? Because clearly he did. It was in what he didn't say as much as what he did.

She wasn't sure if she should ask, but it seemed rather

important considering they kept doing this "are we or aren't we?" dance. "Do you still love her, Jack?"

Stab, stab. "Of course not. I probably didn't love her then, either. I just thought I did."

Hmm. His sharp reply was a glimpse past the slick facade that was Jack Shepard. "You must have, for her to hurt you that way."

He tore open a packet of jam. "It's a long story. Let's just put it this way—the whole thing soured me on thoughts of fairy-tale love for a long time. I mean…I can't say love doesn't exist, because I see it. In my parents, in Callum and Avery, in friends and employees. But it served to make me very, very cautious about putting myself out there."

"Jack Shepard, the risk taker…afraid of love."

"Damn right." Finally he seemed to relax, spread the jam over his toast a little more gently. "Look, I'm perfectly okay with testing my boundaries and capabilities. I'm just not so good with trusting them to other people, know what I mean?"

"So I shouldn't worry about this two-week thing turning into more than a work vacation."

"God, no."

It shouldn't have, but his quick denial hurt.

He put down his knife. "Crap. I didn't mean for it to sound that way, Amy."

"No, clarity is good." Her appetite was all but gone now. Which didn't make sense because that was what she wanted to hear…wasn't it?

He sighed heavily. "This *is* kind of a mess, isn't it?"

When she didn't answer, he touched her hand, prompting her to look up. She didn't want that queer, wonderful turning to happen in her tummy when he gazed into her eyes. Didn't want the awareness of the shape of his lips, the light scent of his aftershave, the other little things that she noticed about him…including the scar beneath his ear.

"I'm not looking for anything past this trip, Amy. You should know that up front. But I think maybe we were fooling ourselves by thinking we could ignore chemistry. We've got it, you and me. Have had since that night on the dance floor. We can try to rationalize it all we want, but it's going to get in our way."

Holy. Mother. Mary. Did he expect her to know how to respond to that?

"The big question is," he continued, "what do we do about it?"

"I, uh…"

"Look at me," he commanded. When she did so, he looked her dead in the eyes. "You are not what they say you are. I can see that. You're skittish as a new colt and blush like an innocent. And news flash—being here with me won't make you what they say, either. The way I see it, we have a choice. We can put on the brakes and stop this right here and right now and stay out of each other's way for the rest of your trip."

Like that had worked so well up to this point.

"Or?"

"Or we enjoy the few weeks and take things as they come. Go in with our eyes wide open. If you're looking for forever, Amy, say no right now. Because I'm not your guy. But if we can go into this knowing exactly what it's not, there's no reason why we shouldn't enjoy each other's company."

"You're suggesting a fling."

"I'm suggesting we stay open to possibilities. As long as we're both aware of what is and isn't on the table."

"Do you run all your negotiations like this?"

He finally smiled again. "Not even close. I'm much tougher with business deals."

Which was why he wasn't just a rancher, but a millionaire a few times over.

"I'm not interested in anything long-term, either," she answered. "I have plans. I don't intend to let a guy get in my way. It's time I started thinking outside the world of Cadence Creek."

"That's not exactly an answer."

She knew that. And she was still considering. Her heart was telling her this was a big mistake. But her head was saying that she could handle it. That she'd look back and regret it if she didn't let herself at least consider the idea of spending a glorious few weeks enjoying the company of Jack Shepard. They had laid out the ground rules. No expectations. No demands.

"I don't know. I kind of liked our plan last night."

"We had a plan?"

She nodded. "On my timetable. I know where you stand, you know where I stand. If either of us changes our minds…no questions asked."

His smile broadened. "Should we shake hands on it?"

"Sure."

She held out her hand, and he took it, but before she could pull it back he turned it over and lifted it, touching his lips to the base of her palm.

Her body went into overdrive.

He let go of her hand. "Now eat. Your breakfast is getting cold and you're going to need your energy for what I have planned this afternoon."

Chapter Six

She hadn't known what to expect when Jack said she'd need her energy for the afternoon. Still, snowshoeing hadn't been remotely on her radar. In all her years in Alberta, she'd never been. She'd stuck to ice-skating at the local rink. Ridden on the back of a snowmobile a time or two. Once her high school friends had taken her skiing in Jasper, and she'd spent the morning taking a lesson and the afternoon sitting in the lodge with a paperback and a large hot chocolate with whip.

It wasn't that she couldn't do outdoor stuff. It was just that she didn't choose to. Not very often.

So standing in the cold, bundled up in a parka, hat, thick mittens and heavy boots while Jack patiently did up the fastenings on a pair of snowshoes, made her feel just a bit like a fish out of water. She was way more an "I like the snow outside but I'm a 'stay inside beside the roaring fire'" kind of person.

"Try that," he suggested, standing up.

The fabric of his jacket made a crinkly noise and Amy looked up. Why on earth did his eyes seem bluer right now? Was it the navy of his jacket, or the piercing clarity of the sky behind them? She slid on her sunglasses, cutting down on the sun-on-snow glare. Jack grinned, the little sideways boyish smile that had the power to melt icicles. "You ready to go?" he asked.

He was already strapped in his snowshoes, and had moved around as easily as if he'd been wearing boots. Meanwhile her feet felt awkward and funny, strapped to the wedgelike contraptions.

"As ready as I'm going to be," she answered. *Please don't let me fall like a newb,* she thought to herself, pulling up her mittens and preparing to take her first step.

"It's a little clunky until you find your stride," Jack suggested. "Don't try to go too fast at first."

"Okay." She pasted on a smile and put her right foot forward, then her left. It felt a bit like an exaggerated walk, with big clown shoes on. A few more steps and she was getting the hang of it. Until she suddenly found herself face-first in the snow, her legs and snowshoes splayed out behind her in a most undignified manner.

Jack's easy laugh touched her ears. She sighed.

A snowshoe appeared beside her right hip, then another on her left, and Jack's mittened hands gripped under her shoulders. "One…two…three…up we go."

It wasn't dignified or graceful, but a few seconds later she was back on her feet, brushing the snow off her coat and ski pants. "You sure you want to take me out there? It could be a very slow trip for you."

"You'll get the hang of it. And it'll be worth it. Trust me."

"Right," she answered, skeptical.

"Come on. Don't let the toes drop. That's what catches and snubs you up."

She concentrated on the movement of the step, adopting the slight spring to the stride that Jack seemed to affect so effortlessly. She wasn't fast, but she managed to get a steady pace going, more intense than walking but definitely easier than a jog in the deep snow.

"You okay?" he asked, slowing until she drew up beside him on the path.

She took a deep breath, noticing that the fresh mountain air held an even more intense scent of pines and evergreens as they made their way into the woods. "I'm okay. It takes some getting used to."

"Easier than walking in the snow and sinking to your thighs," Jack said, staying beside her as they carried on.

"Do you do this often?" she asked, wondering if her legs were going to ache tonight and if she'd have time to check the business email before dinner. There'd only been a scant hour to work in the office before Jack had pulled her away for an afternoon of nature.

"Sometimes I take the horses if the snow's not too deep. And when we have guests, we quite often include a day of snowshoeing or skating. In the summertime, we'll do this as a hike or a trail ride. The view at the end is worth it."

They kept going, sometimes talking, sometimes not, especially when he picked up the pace and Amy's lungs were working overtime as she tried to keep up. Once Jack stopped, he motioned for quiet and reached into his pocket for a baggie. He placed a few pieces of peanut on a log, then dropped a few on the snow, and finally, kept some on the palm of his glove. "Just wait," he said softly, nodding as a black-capped chickadee found the treat on the log. With his voice low, he added, "Look at that trunk. The nuthatches are out."

She saw the light blue bird, its plumage standing out against the grey-brown of the bark. "It's upside down! Weird."

He chuckled. "They walk down the tree headfirst. Cool, right? Now hush. And watch."

Patiently he stood, and after a few minutes the first chickadee perched on his hand, snatching a peanut before darting away.

Once the chickadee had escaped with a treat, the nuthatch found its courage. With a chirp it landed on Jack's hand, cheekily snatched a peanut, chirped again and darted off while Amy laughed.

"Wait. He'll be back. They're pigs once they find out I've got a good supply. Here, come try it."

"I'm sure they won't come to me."

"If you stand still and have food they will. Come here."

She made her way to his side.

"Reach into my pocket for the baggie, and put some on your palm."

She took off her mitten and reached into his pocket. It was toasty warm and her fingers closed over the plastic baggie. She withdrew it and put some bits on the palm of her mitten, then carefully tucked the bag back into his pocket.

"Hold it out and wait."

The nuthatch came back, but perched on Jack's hand with a squawk. It darted off but was back soon after, and hopped from Jack's glove to her mitten.

"Oh, my word."

It snapped up a chunk of peanut, gave a chirp and was gone.

"That's so cool."

A few more birds approached and pecked away at the nuts, growing braver by the moment. Once, when a chickadee was on her palm, a nuthatch flitted past and perched on her hat, waiting for his turn. The bird walked over her head, the tiny feet a peculiar sensation through the knitted fabric. All Amy could think was that she hoped the bird didn't poop on her hat. When she said as much, Jack laughed abruptly, scattering their winged friends into the bushes.

"We should carry on. We've got a ways to go yet."

He reached into his pocket and zipped up the bag of peanuts. "You ready?"

It had been a great chance for her to catch her breath, and she wondered if he'd planned it that way. "I'm good to go. Lead on."

The stride was easier now that she was getting used to it, and twenty minutes later they emerged from the woods into a field, where snow-covered knolls and hills rolled into the distance. The sky was huge, blue with wispy white clouds streaking across it in the mellow afternoon light. In the distance the mountains formed a grey-and-white barrier, tall and proud sentinels guarding the foothills and undulating pastures.

Jack touched her sleeve.

"Come on. Let's sit and have a break."

She followed him to a ridge of large boulders. Some were high and round, not good for sitting, but a few were large and flatter on the top. With quick fingers he undid their snowshoes and then offered her a hand up.

"Isn't it weird that these rocks are just…here? In the middle of your field?"

He laughed. "They're called glacial erratics. Material left behind from the glacier that formed this valley millions of years ago."

"It's hard to imagine this place that long ago, isn't it?"

He shrugged. "Things change over time. Nothing ever stays the same. But while it changes, it somehow stays the same, too. It's one of the things I like about here. It's… constant. There's a permanence to it I like."

He slid a pack off his back. "And now, as a reward for your novice snowshoeing efforts, I have a treat." He undid the zip and pulled out a thermos. "Hot chocolate."

"Oh, that's perfect!" Amy leaned back on her hands and stretched, realizing that her feet felt strangely weightless without the shoes strapped on. The rich scent of chocolate wafted in the air and she accepted the cup gratefully. It was still piping hot, and she sipped it, cupping both hands around the steel mug.

"That's not all." He took out a paper-wrapped package. "Cookies. I grabbed them while we were in town and you were at the post office."

She reached into the bag and pulled out a huge chocolate chip cookie. The first bite was heaven; buttery and chewy and loaded with chocolate chunks.

"I shouldn't eat cookies," she sighed, taking another bite and washing it down with the hot chocolate.

"With all the calories you're burning this afternoon, you can get away with it."

"You bring your clients here?" she asked, breathing deeply. The rest and the refreshments were just the thing to prepare her for the return journey. Maybe she could have done a lot more work, but feeding the birds and sitting on an old rock with Jack Shepard was a darned nice way to spend a few hours.

"Yes. Sometimes just some physical exercise and wideopen space does wonders. No one ever has trouble sleeping when they stay at Aspen Valley. As I mentioned, in the summer we hike it or trail-ride, and it's an easy afternoon activity. In the winter it's snowshoeing." He bit into his own cookie. "I love it here. Stress just seems to melt away. Stress is very small compared to something this big, you know?"

"And were you stressed, Jack?"

He brushed off his hands. "Very. First there was leaving my Olympic dreams behind. And then…well, starting up a new business, then expanding it, took a lot of hours. A lot of agonizing over decisions and money. It was one of my distributors who invited me out here for a few days of R & R. After the third day, I never wanted to leave."

"It suits you. Far better than the confident-businessman image."

"You're not the first to say that."

She wondered who else. And if that person were male or female.

"So why stick with sporting goods?"

"It's a big company. Hard to walk away from. I mean, this place is great and right now it's self-sustaining, but it's not a big income earner. Besides, I do still enjoy it. If I can do both, why not?"

"Doesn't leave you much time for a personal life."

"That hasn't exactly been a priority."

"Do you want to talk about her?"

He balled up the paper bag and shoved it in the pack. "Who?"

"The woman who broke your heart. It was the same year as you hurt your knee, wasn't it?"

His eyebrows shot up. "That was a long time ago." He made it sound like it barely deserved mentioning.

But he'd brought it up earlier. He'd lost the woman he loved and his dreams all in one shot. His safety net, as he'd put it. It was important.

"Doesn't really matter when it was, does it? You still got stomped on."

His gaze darted away and he stared out over the hills. "I was young and naive. I was a different person back then."

"Wow, she must have really done a number on you."

"I was the one who fooled myself into thinking it was more than it was. That it would somehow work out."

Boy, could Amy relate to that. Her one and only relationship had been so short-lived. She'd thought he was wonderful and cared about her the same way. But it had exemplified the cliché of a May–September romance. He'd worked an internship that summer with a local vet before going back to school in the fall. Going back to school and conveniently forgetting all about her.

"When I was nineteen, I met a guy. Terry was working the summer with a local large-animal vet. We spent the whole summer together. He had one year left…one year where we'd have to deal with a long-distance romance. I was game for it. He was my first serious relationship."

"What happened?"

"He went back to school. We had a few phone calls. He emailed me once, but then changed his address because everything came back undeliverable." She shrugged. "So, clearly not as serious as I believed."

"You never heard from him again?"

She shook her head and nudged his arm. "Your turn."

He was quiet for a long moment. "Oh, hell," he finally said, irritation plain in his voice. "It was all over the papers. You probably know the whole story."

She laughed. "Like you can rely on the papers for the truth."

"In this case, they weren't far off. I had an affair with my coach's wife." He frowned. "When you're nineteen, twenty, everything's an adventure. Risk is a thrill, a game. I was full of myself. Was sure we could keep it a secret…. That I was invincible. That I could fix everything. Bulletproof."

There was a long sigh. "I just wanted to get through

the season by keeping it quiet. Then we could go public. I would get another coach and we would be together…."

He zipped up the pack and leaned forward, resting his elbows on his knees. "You weren't the only one who was naive and trusting. The risk was the thrill. But the feelings…they were real. More real than anyone would believe."

"Including her?"

"Especially her."

The sun dipped behind a cloud and the wind shifted, bringing a bitter edge. "We should get back," he suggested, pushing himself off the rock. "Come on, I'll help you get strapped in again."

The carefree mood of earlier was gone. Instead they both seemed more introspective on the hike back through the woods to the ranch house. The forest protected them from the wind once they were back within its shelter, and they passed the spot where they'd fed the birds only an hour earlier. Only a few peanut crumbs remained as they pushed on. As they neared the farmyard, Amy became aware that the afternoon was waning. Dark would soon be upon them. Winter days were short. The light was fleeting and Amy had the strange desire to hang on to every bit of sunlight she could.

To make the most of each day.

Jack had slowed his pace to accommodate hers, and once they were back by the house he quickly undid his snowshoes and then moved to help with hers. She was already kneeling in the snow working on her straps when he dropped to his knee beside her.

"I can manage, Jack."

"Four hands are faster than two. Are you cold?"

Her nose and cheeks were cold and her toes were feeling slightly chilled, but the rest of her was sweating from the exertion. "Not really. My heart rate kept the blood pumping."

He slid the last strap from the buckle. "You go on inside, and I'll put this stuff away."

"See you in a few minutes."

She went inside the warm house and shrugged off her coat and ski pants, leaving her boots on the mat and hanging the rest on hangers in the closet. She went to the kitchen for a drink and saw Jack through the window, carrying the snowshoes to a shed between the house and the barn. She sipped on her glass of water and thought back over the afternoon. The easy way she and Jack had been together, the way they'd laughed while feeding the birds, the thrill that had raced through her at the touch of his hands lifting her up out of the snow.

When they'd first started drinking hot chocolate on the boulder in the field, she'd had a quick thought that maybe he'd kiss her again.

But the conversation had turned serious. Smooth, confident, charismatic Jack had disappeared. Instead he'd let down the walls of charm and self-assurance and she got the feeling she'd had a glimpse of the real Jack Shepard. A man who wasn't as ruthless as his reputation indicated. A man who could break hearts but who had also had his broken.

A man she had more in common with than she'd first thought.

She thought back to what he'd said over breakfast. *If you're looking for forever, Amy, say no right now. Because I'm not your guy.*

She wasn't looking for forever. Not even close. The man she married would have to adore her. He'd have to want to be with her as much as she wanted to be with him. He'd have to respect her dreams and wishes and not just expect her to follow along with his.

She was starting to seriously doubt such a paragon existed.

And Jack was right here. Available. Maybe only for a few weeks. And she wasn't going to fall in love with him. But dammit, it was good to feel like someone saw beneath the surface. That someone understood even a little bit.

Jack shut the door to the shed and started walking back to the house, his long stride eating up the ground, his shoulders hunched against the cold.

The big question was, could she have her few weeks of fun and walk away unscathed? Or should she keep it professional and not take a risk?

BY MIDMORNING JACK could see that Amy was stressed out.

"I never should have taken yesterday afternoon off," she lamented, glasses pushed up her nose as she stared at the computer. "Okay, so the flight comes into the airport at three o'clock and you're meeting it. But there are ten people coming. How are they all getting back here?"

"I have an eight-passenger van in the garage. The SUV seats four more plus the driver. Miguel's taking the passenger van. We've got it covered, Amy. We'll be back here in time for registration and refreshments, and dinner at seven."

"Right. And the chef arrives this afternoon."

"See?" He wasn't the least bit nervous. He'd been through this tons of times before. It was all very relaxed and she'd see that in time.

"I still have to ready the rooms for everyone…."

"You are going to do fine," he said gently, putting a hand on her shoulder.

He shouldn't have touched her. She was already wound

up tight as a spring, and her muscles tensed beneath his fingers. He supposed he should be relieved that she was taking this all so seriously. And yet…he'd been distinctly disappointed when she'd claimed fatigue last night, and had disappeared for a bath and bed.

He should never have said anything about Sheila. Talk about a mood killer.… Plus he knew what it said about him that he'd fallen for a married woman. Even though things weren't as black-and-white as they seemed to the casual observer, putting himself in the middle of that volatile situation had been wrong.

He knew exactly what Amy meant when she said people had long memories. Even if he'd changed, he would never live that down. Never forgive himself.…

He slid his hand off her shoulder and stepped back. "I'll let you get to it. Is there anything I can do to help?"

"The activity tomorrow. Do we need a waiver for that?"

"No. That's covered by the company running it."

"Okay. And New Year's Eve…"

Right. He'd forgotten that the group would be here that night. They should have something special. Food and drinks. Music. Party hats.

"Damn. I totally forgot. I'll handle it, Amy."

"You mean between horseback rides and dogsledding and skiing and anything else you've got planned?"

"It shouldn't be left up to you."

She let out a huge sigh. "One thing at a time. I need to make a list, and then stick to it. Jack, if you can make sure that the spare outerwear is organized that would be great. Just in case people forget mittens, ski pants, that sort of thing. I'll get the rooms ready and show the chef around when he arrives. Plan for drinks and snacks at five."

She got out a pad of paper and began jotting down

items. As he watched, the list got longer and longer until it was nearly to the bottom of the notepad.

Then she began numbering them—in order of priority.

She wasn't kidding. She didn't look the type, but the girl was super organized. He wondered how she reacted when a monkey wrench got thrown into the situation. Cool control, or did her well-ordered plan fall to pieces?

"Take a breath," he commanded, and turned her chair so she was facing away from the desk and looking up at him instead. "Relax. Everything will get done."

She bit down on her lip. He couldn't help it; his gaze dropped to where the pink fullness was pressed by her teeth. He forced himself to look away and found himself staring into her eyes. It wasn't just the volume of work she was unsure about, was it? There was something more at work.

"What's really making you nervous?" he asked. He braced his hands on the arms of the chair, making it impossible for her to duck away. "What are you truly worried about?"

"You're wasting time, Jack, and I have work to do."

"You've got lots of time. I'd like an answer." He kneeled down a bit so their eyes were level. "I can't help you if I don't know what's really freaking you out."

There was a long pause as she considered. A long pause in which their gazes held and she seemed to be testing him—though for what, he wasn't sure.

"What if they don't like me?"

She put her feet flat on the floor and pushed, sliding the rolling chair out of his grasp. "Oh, man, that sounds so stupid outside my head."

"That's what you're worried about? But that's silly. You're one of the most likable people I've ever met. You're very good with people."

"But this is different. This group who is arriving... they're executives from some Fortune 500 company and I'm used to flower arrangements for Joe down the road who doesn't know an orchid from an alstroemeria."

Ah. He got it now. "Amy Wilson, you are just as good as anyone who walks through that door. Don't let a title or a bank balance intimidate you. Underneath we're all people. And the measure of a person has little to do with what name is on their door or the size of their 401(k)."

"Easy for you to say. You are one of those people."

He frowned. Was this why she kept backing off each time they got close? Because she was intimidated by his...his what? His success? His bank account? Sure, he'd worked hard and he was used to fine things when he wanted them. Like the chartered jet. Like the luxury SUV in the driveway. But that wasn't all he was. Not when you got beneath the surface.

Except that was generally off-limits. On purpose.

The problem with Amy Wilson was that he really couldn't figure her out at all. She could flirt like a champ but he got the impression she was more innocent than she appeared. She was extremely personable and yet insecure, very capable but also unsure of her abilities.

"Look," he said quietly, "this place—Aspen Valley— it's about stripping away all the superficial layers and leveling the playing field. No one is more important than anyone else. I don't want to hear another word about you feeling inferior, you got that? You're as good as the rest of 'em. And they are going to love you. All you have to do is smile your beautiful smile and you'll have them in the palm of your hand."

"Like I have you?" she asked, skepticism rife in her voice.

"Like you have me," he confirmed.

"Jack…"

"Why'd you disappear last night?" he asked. He hadn't been planning to. He'd told himself to let it go.

"Because I had to think. I needed time to think about whether or not I can walk away from this in a few weeks and be okay. I meant what I said at breakfast. I should keep my distance now."

"So you were avoiding me."

She smiled, just a little. "I had a glass of wine and a hot bath and a good night's sleep, which was just what the doctor ordered."

"And did you come to any conclusions?"

"I didn't. I like you, Jack. I like you a lot. And everything you said yesterday made perfect sense. You were honest and I appreciate that. Clearly there's something between us. But taking that sensible approach and applying it to reality…that's where I'm struggling. And until I know for sure, I'm going to play it safe." She looked down. "I'm not a risk taker, Jack. I like to pretend I am, but I'm really not. If I were, I wouldn't be where I am in my life."

Jack stared down at her. Wisdom. He hadn't expected wisdom from her. With her hair up in a little twist and her glasses perched on the bridge of her nose, she looked beautiful, and smart, and irresistible.

He stood, keeping his hands on the arms of her chair. Then he leaned forward and touched his lips to hers. She responded, not with the flame of passion but with a soft sigh that affected nearly the same result. God, she was sweet. Sweeter than she realized. Sweeter than he deserved for sure.

"The ball's in your court," he said, though it pained him to say it. He was used to going after what he wanted and getting it and the hell with whatever stood in his way.

He wasn't the kind to step back and wait for opportunity to come to him. But this wasn't business. And she wasn't the usual type that hung around waiting for their chance. He could see right through those types. Amy was different, and he felt the need to be careful with her.

Come to think of it, he always had. Ever since that first night when he took her home from the wedding and spent an hour visiting with his parents rather than taking her up to his room. There'd been this intuitive need to look after her.

She ran her tongue over her lower lip and he nearly reconsidered. Nearly pushed his case. He would probably win.

Instead he backed up another step. "On your time. When you're ready. You know where I am," he said.

She nodded.

And he got out of there before he changed his mind.

Chapter Seven

Amy stood in the middle of the empty foyer, feeling like a tornado had blown through and had now left her with the aftermath.

Since exactly 4:07 p.m. yesterday afternoon, it had been chaos. Fun chaos, but hectic just the same. She had been on hand to greet guests and show them to their rooms—rooms she'd spent two hours in the afternoon making sure were perfectly spotless. Then it had been back to the kitchen to help the chef—a lovely man in his forties named Chuck—with the refreshment prep. Together she and Jack opened bottles of wine, beer and sparkling water for the new guests and she served Chuck's delicious refreshments in the living room before a blazing fire and lit-up Christmas tree. Bacon-wrapped jalapeños, "cowboy caviar" and chips, grilled shrimp and potato skins had rounded out the prefeast, only to be followed a few hours later by a gorgeous beef tenderloin, roasted carrots and garlic mashed potatoes.

It had been late when she'd finally put the kitchen to rights and made sure everyone had what they needed before turning in.

This morning she'd been up at six and was showered and ready when Chuck arrived at seven for the break-fast meal. He put Amy to work as a sous-chef, scramble-frying sausage while he made drop biscuits. Then he had her make a fruit salad with honey and mint while he made a milk gravy with the sausage and drippings. Coffee and juice rounded out the meal and at eight everyone was seated in the dining room, eating happily and talking about their plans for the day. First up, a two-hour horseback ride with Miguel, Raffy and Jack along as guides.

Being more of an indoor girl, Amy should have been relieved that she didn't have to go along. But hearing Jack talk about the ranch, and how the ride would give them a tour of the cattle operation, she wished she could.

Never mind that she'd hardly been able to say two words to Jack since their arrival. As the group prepared for their ride, Amy finally got time to sit at the breakfast nook with a plate of biscuits and gravy before starting the meal cleanup. She'd barely finished eating when Chuck asked for her help again with preparing lunch. She arranged a platter of homemade chocolate chip cookies while Chuck built sandwiches from the leftover tenderloin and sourdough bread. Another tray of vegetables and dip was put in the fridge—all Amy had to do at noon was serve it.

Now, finally, it was ten-thirty, Chuck was gone until it was time for dinner, the dishes were washed and put away, the dishwasher running, and the house was utterly silent.

There was still housekeeping to do. And she should spend an hour or so in the office....

By the time everyone arrived back at twelve, Amy was feeling run off her feet. Still, she pasted on a smile, took a deep breath and put out the platters of food for a casual lunch.

Jack found her in the kitchen, half of her sandwich

abandoned on the counter as she unloaded the clean dishes from the dishwasher. "Doing okay?"

She smiled and kept stacking plates. "Sure."

"I thought you'd eat with us."

She bit back a sharp answer—it wouldn't exactly be helpful and she was wondering if Rosa had been this rushed or if she'd handled things with more ease. "Oh, just trying to stay ahead of the work," she replied.

"It's a lot, but it's only for a few days. Then things settle down again before the next lot arrive."

"I'm doing okay. Really."

"Good. Because I'm stealing you away for the afternoon."

She sighed. "Jack, I really do have enough to keep me busy here."

"I'll help you load up the dishwasher. Put the leftovers in the fridge and put on a parka. You're not going to want to miss it."

She knew the schedule. And she was tempted. Today the group was doing something that Amy had never done before. They were going dogsledding.

"Jack…"

He came over and grabbed the cutlery tray, went to the drawer and started unloading it. "You're here to have some fun, too. Chuck will be here to get dinner. Tonight will be an earlier night, because everyone will be exhausted from their day outdoors. Everything's gone great so far. Come on, Amy. It'll be fun. It's like flying on snow."

His eyes sparkled at her. She was helpless when he looked at her like that, all expectant and enthusiastic. "You're sure there's room for me?"

"You can drive the SUV and follow me there. See? Still working."

She raised an eyebrow at him…. Being a chauffeur wasn't exactly hard work. But she did want to go. Wanted to experience new things.

"What about the office work?"

He shut the drawer and faced her. "It'll keep. Unless there's something urgent, admin can wait until our guests are gone. Rosa usually catches up when the house is quiet. Now, do you have any more excuses?"

She shook her head.

"Good. Be ready in half an hour."

She hurriedly tidied the kitchen and grabbed her coat, hat and mitts. The rest of the group was getting dressed, and she noticed they were joking and laughing more than last night, which had felt a little like a cocktail party, slightly more poised and formal. As a group they were becoming more relaxed with each other.

She followed Jack out the lane and onto the main road, heading away from the ranch and toward the base of the mountains. It was only ten, maybe fifteen minutes when he turned off and led her up a gradual incline, past a sign that announced Dogsled Adventure Trails. The trees broke into a clearing, and Jack parked the van to one side while Amy pulled in beside him.

The sound was unreal.

Barks and yips filled the air as a group of guides hooked dogs to harnesses. Amy watched as a man with a ginormous beard invited the guests to meet another group of dogs, all bouncing feet and wagging tails. It smelled…very doggy. One whole side of the yard was kennels. A teenager worked to one side, scooping out a few empty areas. Doggy it might be, but Amy could see that amidst the chaos was a precise routine.

Jack came over and took her arm. "Come on. You should meet a few of these guys. They're dying to run today." He led her to a small group, where a pair of Alaskan huskies were getting attention. "This is Barnum and Bailey. Say hello."

Delighted, she kneeled down and offered her hand for a sniff. Immediately they rubbed up against her mitt, bundles of pent-up energy ready to hit the trails. "John says these two will be on the final run of the day," Jack explained. "They don't get to go this time."

"I bet they feel bad about that. They look like they'd go like the wind."

"You have no idea." He nodded at the sleds lined up for passengers. "Generally each sled will take three adults, but because there are twelve of us, we're pairing up."

Amy nodded. "There are three sleds."

"We're going in two separate groups. You and I will go with the first group, while the others stay back and learn about the dogs and the operation. Then we'll do the same when the second group is out."

"Just you and me?" Her heart gave a little thump.

"Yes, just us. I don't always go along, but I thought today I'd go with you. See what you think. Spend some time hanging out together."

It was hard to come up with a reasonable argument. Plus he'd stayed true to his word and hadn't pressured her in any way. He'd left it all firmly in her court, just as he'd said. She was starting to realize that Jack kept his promises.

"Let's go, then," she said, a little bit of excitement fizzing through her veins. After the hard work of the past twenty-four hours, it felt like an extravagant treat. Plus it was something she'd never done before. And wasn't this trip all about trying new things?

Minutes later she found herself tucked in the sled, cushioned between Jack's legs and both of them covered with the sled bag. The dogs vibrated with restrained energy; the guide stepped on the runners behind them. Amy could feel the weight of him there, felt the moment he put his hands firmly on the driver's bow.

"You ready?" Jack's voice was warm in her ear and she shivered as she nodded.

There was a shout and a feeling of release and then they were moving.

It wasn't as smooth as Amy expected. As the dogs started off, the sled bumped and banged over lumps in the trail, and her stomach did a flip when they built up momentum and went over a dip. She laughed out loud, feeling the sting of snow on her cheeks as they left the yard behind and slid deep into the surrounding forest.

"Okay?" Jack's voice rumbled at her ear again.

"More than okay," she replied. "You were right. It feels like we're flying!"

He laughed. She felt the rise and fall of his chest against her back, the warmth of his body cushioning hers, the long length of his legs riding along her thighs. Now that they were underway, the dogs had stopped barking and simply raced them over the snow, the runners making a squeaky slide against the white trail. The crisp air was tangy with the evergreen scent and Amy leaned her head back against his shoulder.

His hands, even though they were encased in thick mittens, slid around her ribs and held her close. In that moment there was nowhere else she'd rather be.

They were on a dogsled, wrapped up in heavy winter clothing, and still his touch burned through to her skin. She shifted slightly, her bottom wiggling in the V of his legs, and she heard a quick intake of breath. His hands moved, skimming over her hips, firm and warm.

And a driver was behind them, who could, in all likelihood, see inside the sled bag, at least partially.

She diverted herself from the feel of Jack's body—or attempted to—by asking questions about the dogs. Where they came from, how many to a team, how many times they ran a day. The team slowed to a trot as the driver chatted, and they skimmed more slowly over the path, a break in the woods that was maybe only a foot wider than the sled on either side.

After about forty-five minutes, the path widened and opened up into a meadow that overlooked a lake, the frozen surface cold and rigid.

"Look," he said, "about two o'clock."

Together Jack and Amy looked to their right. A bull moose stood proudly in the middle of the meadow, a smaller cow nearby. They were totally unconcerned with the dogs, and the dogs weren't the least bit interested in them, either. Instead they raced over the snow, the dogs picking up the pace on the wide-open stretch. When they got close to the moose, the animals lumbered off in their awkward yet somehow graceful gait.

"Awesome, right?"

"Very," she answered. Despite the heavy clothing and protection of the sled covering, the tips of her ears and nose were growing cold. She burrowed her face into the fleecy inside of her coat and Jack's arms tightened around her.

When they finally entered the yard, the next teams of dogs were being hooked to the harnesses and the guests were hovering around, anxious to get going. They came to a halt and the sled bag was unzipped, releasing Amy and Jack from their cozy cocoon. His hand gave a slight squeeze to her thigh before she slid out into the brisk winter air.

They were separated in the commotion of the return-
ing teams and the exclamations of the guests who had
already completed their runs. When Amy looked over
again, Jack was laughing and talking to the head of the
group, the company's CEO. The man looked as unbusi-
nesslike as she could imagine—his hat askew, puffy
jacket, cheeks ruddy from the cold. He looked just like
the rest of the people there, and she supposed that was
the point.

A team.

She went to the office, housed out of the cabin on-site,
and paid the invoice with a check that Jack had signed.
When she returned to the yard, Jack was waiting for her.

"I was wondering…can you find your way back to
the ranch?"

"I think so."

He put his hand under her elbow as they walked slowly
away from the cabin and toward where the vehicles were
parked. "There are a few guests who would like to return
rather than hang around for another hour. You can check
on Chuck and I thought maybe they'd like to relax in the
hot tub before dinner. It's been a long day, and they might
be a little saddle sore from this morning."

The idea of the hot tub was tempting, though Amy
would prefer it be à deux rather than a group activity.

He took a business card out of his pocket. "Have you
got a pen?"

She'd left her pack in the SUV, so together they walked
to the vehicle and she grabbed a pen from the side pouch.
Quickly he scribbled a rough map on the reverse side of
the card.

"If you're unsure, this will help. I'll see you back there,
okay?"

"We probably won't be more than three quarters of

an hour ahead of you," she said. "If people are ready to go, I'll drive them."

The four others who'd gone on the first run were ready, so within a few moments they were all loaded in the SUV and Amy was making her way down the lane at a crawl. She checked the rearview mirror and saw Jack give a wave, and she waved back. The conversation in the car was light—Jack was right, people were getting tired. A hot meal, a soak in a hot tub—it would be just the thing after the day in the outdoors.

She headed out the drive, turned onto the main road and tried to remember how long they'd driven on the way there before turning. She guessed about ten minutes....

Fifteen minutes later she admitted to herself that she was lost. Nothing looked familiar, not a road sign or any landscape.

And the CEO was sitting in the backseat.

She turned around in a driveway and retraced her steps, but after a few minutes she was no closer to knowing where she was than before. The crude map on the business card was no help. As each second ticked past, she felt more and more like an incompetent idiot.

"Miss Wilson?" The woman beside her looked worried. "Shouldn't we be back by now?"

Amy tried a nervous laugh. "Well, funny you should mention that. It appears I'm a bit...directionally challenged."

"We're lost?"

"Well...I wouldn't quite go that far. I think I just missed the turnoff to the ranch." At this rate, Jack would be back before she would.

And she'd look like a dimwit. Even more than she already did.

She pasted on what she hoped was an encouraging

smile. "I remember passing this garage before we got to the dogsled place, so I'm going to turn around and head back again. Everyone keep their eyes peeled, okay? For a familiar turnoff." She slowed for the turn. "Sorry, everyone. I just arrived a few days ago. I'm not as familiar with the area as I hoped."

She was back on the main road again, heading toward town. The chatter in the car, the easy conversation about the dogsled experience disappeared, leaving an uncomfortable silence. More signs appeared along the roadside as they got closer and closer to town and farther away from the ranch. Amy blinked several times as tears of humiliation blurred her vision. She should have paid better attention during the drive out, rather than focusing simply on Jack's taillights.

"Anyone want a coffee?" A familiar coffee shop appeared on the right. "I'll give Jack a call while we're stopped. My treat, of course."

She parked and everyone got out. When they all had hot cups of coffee in hand, she went outside to the parking lot and took out her cell.

This was exactly the kind of thing she'd been afraid of. Screwing up. Especially with Jack depending on her. The one person who didn't seem to buy in to what everyone else thought. He just hadn't known her long enough, had he?

Dread settling in the pit of her stomach, she dialed the phone.

"Amy?"

He didn't even bother with hello. She closed her eyes. "Hey."

"Where on earth are you? Are you okay? We just got back to the house. You should have been here ages ago!"

"I got lost."

There was a beat of silence, but it was enough for Amy to feel the disappointment.

"Do you know where you are?"

"I'm in town. I stopped at a coffee shop and bought everyone a coffee." She swallowed. "I'm sorry, Jack. I thought I remembered the way back. I turned around a couple of times and tried again, but nothing seemed familiar."

Jack sighed and she felt even worse.

"Did you try using the GPS?"

Oh. My. God.

Could she feel any more stupid? "There's a GPS in the car." It wasn't a question. It was a statement, a confirmation of her own ineptitude.

"The touch screen in the middle of the dashboard. If I'd thought you'd have trouble, I'd have suggested it instead of writing on that card."

"I'm not good with directions, apparently." The words sounded bitter.

"Don't be so hard on yourself. You're not familiar with the area at all. I should have suggested using it in the first place. I'm so used to driving here, it never crossed my mind."

"I'll get back in and bring it up on the screen."

"There's a preset called Home. Just put that in and you'll be fine."

"I'm sorry, Jack."

"Oh, hell, don't worry about it. I'm just glad you're okay and everyone's accounted for. I'll see you in a bit?"

"Yeah."

She went back to the car and turned on the ignition so that the screen lit up. She found the GPS button and a map instantly popped up. A few presses later and she found the presets, and pressed Home.

A line popped up on the screen, following a road on the map.

Could she be more incompetent?

With the help of the GPS, she got her passengers back to the ranch within twenty minutes. Embarrassed, she slipped into the kitchen to work on dinner prep, the easiest way she could think of to remain invisible. Chuck was there but said nothing about her late arrival. He just had her slice dinner rolls and grate cabbage for slaw while he slipped cobs of corn into boiling water. Tonight the group would be treated to ribs basted with a rich barbecue sauce, homemade baked beans and corn. When the corn was in the pot, Chuck turned his attention to the warm custard sauce he was making to go with the caramel bread pudding for dessert.

She'd switched to grating carrots when Jack came into the kitchen. He looked amazing, Amy thought. He'd changed on his arrival back home and now wore faded jeans and a knitted sweater. His hair was damp and curled around his collar—had he had a soak in the hot tub, as well? She thought of him wearing nothing but swim trunks and easing into the steaming hot water and her pulse began hammering.

"You disappeared after you got back."

She shrugged and focused her gaze back on the grater. "Licking my wounds."

His low chuckle rode along her nerve endings. She slid a sideways glance at Chuck, but the chef was more concerned with whisking his egg yolks than he was with Amy and Jack.

"It could have happened to anyone. You're not familiar. I should have set up the GPS for you from the start."

"I thought I could handle it. I wanted to handle it. To…"

She broke off, frowned, grated the knob of carrot harder. "To what?"

"To prove to you I could. And instead I messed up."

"Everyone got back okay. And one of the ladies—Lisa, I think—said how cool you were and how nice it was for you to spring for coffee. No one was upset, Amy."

"They were awfully quiet in the car."

"It's been a long day for them. If you were out there—" he gestured toward the main part of the house with a thumb "—you'd see it's pretty low-key."

She wanted to believe him, but found it difficult. "It's not just that."

"Then what?"

She gave a sidelong glance at Chuck. He was still standing at the stove, seemingly paying little attention, but she knew he could hear every word. She grabbed Jack's sleeve and pulled him over toward the pantry.

"I disappointed you, after I promised to handle things," she murmured. "I know getting lost with your guests doesn't look good. It shouldn't reflect badly on you."

He laughed a little. "Good grief. It was a detour. You think things don't happen when the rest of us are here? You just roll with it. No one was hurt. At the very worst, it was a slight inconvenience. Certainly not worth you being so upset."

She looked up into his eyes. "You're sure?"

"Of course I'm sure. You're helping me out of a bind. It'd be foolish to think we're not going to hit a wrinkle or two."

She wasn't sure he would be able to convince her that it was no big deal, but she suspected that was because she felt stupid not just for getting lost, but because she hadn't clued in that the vehicle had a GPS. In her defense, she'd never been able to afford a car with that option, so it hadn't crossed her mind. It simply didn't occur to her to think about satellite radio and heated seats and all the other options that came standard on a luxury vehicle.

"Give yourself a break," he suggested, leaning in and pressing a brotherly kiss to her forehead. "And go change. Put on something comfortable and come have dinner with us. Tonight is movie night. It's going to be very quiet and relaxed."

"I don't know…"

"Up to you. But I'm guessing a movie and a glass of wine might be a nice way to spend an evening."

It might be. If it were just the two of them. And then maybe they could take advantage of the hot tub….

But there were ten other people. And since Jack had backed off, it meant it was up to her to make a move. Amy was a lot of things, but she knew she wasn't that brave. And despite the day's mishap, she wasn't that stupid, either.

Chapter Eight

Jack kept his distance from the office. Amy was in there catching up on admin and he wasn't in the mood for any one-on-one time. It was too dangerous. He'd promised to leave things in her court but it was getting more difficult with each passing day. Yesterday she'd declined the day of cat skiing with the group, insisting she was too much of a novice and that backcountry powder skiing wasn't her thing. He hadn't pushed it. She'd stayed behind and run things like clockwork. To make up for the previous day's gaff, he was certain.

This morning he found himself out in the barn, oiling the tack for the sleigh ride this afternoon, making sure nothing was cracked or worn, even though he knew that Miguel would have gone over it already.

He'd been so alarmed when he'd arrived home from the dogsledding and she hadn't been here. Worse when he realized that he didn't have her cell phone number. Hearing the phone ring had been such a relief.

In the space of a few minutes, he'd told himself quite rationally that it couldn't have been an accident because they would have seen it on the way home. The irrational part of him knew that they would be invisible if they'd gone down an embankment. He'd convinced himself that they were lost, or had taken a side trip into town. Both of which ended up being correct....

The scariest thing had been the rush of relief he'd felt seeing her get out of the vehicle. Yes, he'd worried about their clients but it was different with Amy. And that was bad. That was very bad. He cared, but he was starting to care too much.

It was just as well she wasn't here for much longer, wasn't it? Before he really got into trouble.

He had wanted to get back in the van and go looking for her. To ride to her rescue. The last time he'd done that he'd ended up losing his heart to a woman who had stomped on it. He'd offered everything and she had turned it away.

Amy seemed very sweet, but she was stubborn. She was going back to Canada. Their paths would rarely cross....

Except they would. Because Callum was there. Because the lodge he'd just bought was there.

Hell, she didn't even know about that new development.

His head kept telling him to steer clear. But every time he found himself in a room with her, he conveniently forgot. It wasn't that he wanted her too much to think straight, though wanting her was definitely an issue. It was more that he simply enjoyed being with her. Talking to her. Hanging out with her. It was comfortable and easy. When he was with her he stopped being Jack Shepard, former athlete; Jack Shepard, sporting goods mogul; Jack Shepard, millionaire.

He was Jack Shepard, ordinary guy. A man who liked the outdoors. A man who didn't feel he needed to apologize for trading Armani for Levi's. The unvarnished truth of it was he liked himself better when he was around her. She had no idea how unique that made her. How dangerous....

Miguel came wandering through the barn, his boots scuffing on the concrete. "Hey, boss. What's up?"

"Not much. Group's having a meeting inside, so I thought I'd check the tack for this afternoon."

"Just did it myself yesterday. Figured you'd want it done for the sleigh ride."

"Yeah."

"Stuff on your mind?"

Miguel had no idea.

"How's Rosa?" Jack asked.

"Coming home later this afternoon. Raffy helped me move her bed downstairs. It'll be good to have her home."

"You sure you've got someone to stay with her?"

"Positive. And I promise to let you know if I need some time off."

Jack nodded.

"So, what's got you so worked up you're out here cleaning tack?"

"Why does that mean I'm worked up?"

Miguel laughed. "Amigo, when I find you hiding out in the barn alone, I figure you've got your thinking cap on."

Jack shrugged.

"Woman troubles?"

Jack shrugged again, not wanting to answer.

Miguel pulled up a bench. "This have something to do with the lady you've got filling in for Rosa?"

He angled a sharp look at Miguel. "Why would you say that?"

"Saw you out on snowshoes the other day. Caught a good look at her, too. She's a pretty one."

"She's all right."

Miguel laughed again and slapped Jack's knee. "You're kidding me, right? All those blond curls and that figure? I hope that's what has you tied up in knots. If it isn't, I might start worrying about you."

Jack couldn't help the small smile that crept up his cheek.

"Listen, Jack. Not every woman out there is Sheila. She used you. She was…broken. It was never going to be a good situation."

"I have a tendency to want to fix what's broken, Miguel. You ever notice that?"

"Like with her? With this place?"

"Yeah. Just like that."

"It's not a bad quality, son. If not for that, me, Rosa, Raffy, the other hands…we'd all be out of work."

Jack dropped his head, the tack idle in his hands. "It's not necessarily a good trait, either."

There was quiet for a moment.

"People are going to disappoint you all through this life, Jack. What has you so afraid?"

The answer wasn't difficult. "I don't trust it. She could hurt me, Miguel, if I let her."

"Good."

"What?" Jack lifted his head in surprise. How could it possibly be a good thing that someone had that much power over him after all this time?

"Good," Miguel repeated. "I've spent the last few years wondering if you'd ever care about anyone enough to let them in. People only get so far with you and then you shut them out."

"Clearly I haven't done so well with that in regard to you."

Miguel chuckled at what Jack was implying. "Oh, you did at first. It was all about the ranch, and how much you loved it, and how much you needed it. You needed it more than it needed you. This place isn't going anywhere. It can't hurt you, so it's safe. Rosa and me…we just came with the package."

It hurt to have their relationship put in such a plain way. "That's not true. You and Rosa…you're family."

"We are now. You're our family, too. Which is why I'm going to offer you this advice. Why does this girl mean so much? Is it because she needs you? Or do you need her?"

Jack resumed polishing, setting up an easy rhythm. "Heavy questions considering I've only known her for a couple of weeks."

Miguel snorted. "I knew Rosa was the one for me the first time I asked her to dance and she stomped on my foot. Don't close this door, Jack. The only way you're going to know if it's real is to let it be real. Whatever happens, happens."

"She stayed with him, Miguel. After all he'd done. After all we'd planned…" He stared off into space. "She stayed with him and watched when he…"

His throat closed over and he couldn't finish the sentence. Miguel knew exactly who he was talking about. Jack could still see the hatred and rage in his coach's eyes. Still feel the searing pain in his skull as fist struck bone and things went temporarily black.

"Chase was a bastard," Miguel confirmed. "But you were hardly more than a kid. You've got to let it go, son. You've got to stop being angry."

Jack sighed. "I know."

"Maybe this girl can help with that."

"Amy. Her name is Amy."

Miguel patted his leg again. "Well, I need to be getting on. What time do you want the sleigh ready?"

"Two?"

"Sounds good."

Miguel paused at the door. "Hey, it's New Year's Eve. Tomorrow's a brand-new year. Might be a good time to, you know, make a change."

"I don't believe in resolutions."

"Neither do I, son," Miguel said, his hand on the door frame. "Neither do I."

Jack heard Miguel's boots echo back down the hall. He picked up another piece of harness and began working in some conditioner. It was easy for Miguel to say.

It wasn't just that he'd fallen in love with Sheila. Or that he'd promised to take her away from Chase at the end of the season. It was that she'd stood by when they were discovered and stayed silent. How she'd watched as Chase threw the first punch, and the second, and the third. She'd insisted he go home instead of calling the doctor....

He never should have gone on the training run. Never should have pretended he was okay when he had a concussion. Because all it took was a single moment of dizziness and the life he'd wanted was over.

He was older and wiser now and knew that the mistakes of the past had led him to where he was now, and his life was pretty great.

But it had come at a price. And it was a cost he could never forget.

AMY DUMPED THE shopping bags on the counter and let out a huge breath. Jack had left the planning of New Year's Eve up to her, and she was determined that it was going to be great. She'd been at a loss about what to do until late last night, just before falling asleep.

And it hadn't been a cheap trip into town. She'd bought out the houseware section's supply of fondue pots and oil, not to mention cheese, dips and all the other necessities. But really, as far as Amy was concerned, tonight the ranch house would be transformed into a mountain getaway. While she did feel a bit guilty running up Jack's credit card, all the equipment would stay with the business.

She asked Chuck's advice as he did up the lunch prep—something he called Chuckwagon Chili—and she took over half the butcher block and began chopping. When everything was stored in the fridge, she served lunch. Then there was cleanup, and she wondered how she was ever going to make it to midnight without keeling over from exhaustion.

Jack found her on the back porch, stowing the champagne since there was no room in the fridge. "Interesting refrigeration technique," he commented, and she straightened.

"It's fairly mild today. I should be able to leave it all right, and with everything in the fridge for tonight…"

"What did you end up planning, anyway?"

She chafed her arms. "Let's go inside. It's a nice temperature for champagne, but not so much for me without a jacket."

They went back into the kitchen and she shivered as Jack shut the door. "Brr," she said, hugging her arms close.

"You should have put on a coat." Jack came over and rubbed her upper arms. It was meant to be efficient and platonic with no motive or subtext, she was sure. But it was still his hands on her. Even without the brisk rubbing, her body would have warmed up. This staying away from him was proving quite difficult. Especially since he seemed determine to honor his pledge to leave it up to her. It was meant to make her feel comfortable and in control. All it did was make her flip-flop constantly on what she wanted.

And right now his hands felt so good....

She smiled and made herself take a step back. "I got the idea of a fondue. Everyone can mingle, it's different, and it seemed...I don't know, like a perfect wintertime way to end the day after a sleigh ride."

"Bringing a bit of the Alps to the west?"

She shrugged. "I went to Banff once and had fondue at this place. It was fun. And delicious. I'm not a chef, so if left to me it would have been purchased trays from the supermarket and drinks."

"It sounds fun. But I don't think Rosa ever had any fondue pots in the kitchen."

She felt her cheeks heat a little. "I used your card and bought them. I figured you could keep them on hand for other events."

He raised an eyebrow. "Look at you, stepping in and making decisions."

Oh, goodness, she supposed she really should have asked first. "I'm sorry, Jack. Should I take them back?" There was still the afternoon. She could pick something else up for food, and surely Chuck would think of something to do with the cubed meat and veggies in the fridge.

"It wasn't a criticism. I appreciate the initiative. It sounds like fun. It might actually make a nice icebreaker event for future groups. It's very social."

"You're okay with it, then?"

A hint of a dimple appeared on his cheek. "I am. I just like winding you up a bit, that's all."

Huh. She could do with some good winding up....

Being so close to him and not touching really was starting to take a toll, she thought. And she wondered—not for the first time—if she were being a little silly about it. After all, she was a grown woman with her eyes wide open. Now that she was out of Cadence Creek she realized that her plan for the future was actually a good one. Her mom seemed to be doing okay in her absence, which took a huge load off Amy's mind.

She'd needed to broaden her horizons. And here was a handsome man standing before her who had admitted he was attracted to her, who wasn't making any demands, who was refreshingly honest about where he stood....

And she was too scared to make the first move. Wouldn't the old gossips back home get a kick out of that?

"Well, I'm glad you agree," she responded, letting her breath out slowly. "Was there anything you needed? I was just about to go finish up with the housekeeping upstairs. The trip to town put me behind."

"We're leaving on our sleigh ride in an hour. I thought you'd like to join us."

"I should probably stay in and get things ready." She said the responsible thing, though a sleigh ride on New Year's Eve afternoon sounded idyllic.

"There will be time to get things ready. Chuck said he is preparing a light meal for dinner because of the party later, and the Christmas decorations are still up. What more do you need? We'll be back by four."

She really only needed an hour or so to set up the fondue stations and put out the few decorations she'd bought. That would still leave her time to get ready for the party.

"I don't expect to be treated to all the fun stuff the same as your paying guests, that's all." She looked up at him. "I came to work, you know?"

"And you are, and you're doing a great job. But the deal was also to give you a new experience for a few weeks. Let me do that. Come with us. There's hot chocolate laced with Irish cream in it for you. And the best views in Montana." He came closer and she felt her eyes open wider. It would take nothing at all for her to reach out and rest her fingers on his chest. To close the meager gap between them.

"Besides," he said softly, "I hate sitting up in that front seat all alone."

"So you're just looking for a sled bunny," she replied, surprised at how soft and husky her voice sounded in the large kitchen.

"Company," he corrected, and she might have felt brushed-off, except his gaze swept down her body and back up again, heating her from head to toe.

"I might be able to spare a few hours."

"Great. We're going to meet at the main doors to the barn. Dress warm."

"Yes, sir," she answered. "Now if you'll excuse me, dirty linens await."

"What an exciting life you lead," he teased. Then with a wink, he said, "See you later."

She watched him walk out the door, all cool confidence and sexiness. What on earth was she protecting herself from?

The answer came readily enough. It was old habits. She had a tendency to see any new relationship as "the one." Jack wasn't. They were both clear on that.

Well, it was time for her to start some new habits. And Jack seemed like a very willing volunteer....

The sleigh was ready and waiting, the horses shifting impatiently from one hoof to the other as the group mingled around the barn. The mood was definitely light and celebratory, with the guests chatting and laughing before climbing aboard. Blanket-lined benches ran up each side of the sleigh with more blankets stacked at the front for extra warmth. But the day, while cold, wasn't frigid and the sun was shining brightly, warming the back of Amy's jacket.

"You made it." Jack came out of the barn, pulling on heavy leather gloves. He wore a black Stetson—the first time she'd ever seen him in a cowboy hat—and she caught her breath. He looked taller, more rugged if that were even possible. His heavy jacket had sheepskin at the collar. The Cadence Creek men wore similar outerwear every day of their blessed lives, but it had never looked like *that*.

"I did." She smiled up at him. "Just made it, from the looks of things."

"We're ready to go," he agreed, and moved toward the back of the sleigh. "Okay, everyone, let's board up and get this show on the road!"

"He's a handsome devil, isn't he?"

Amy turned at the sound of a clearly admiring voice. One of the group's attendees stood beside her, a woman in her early forties if Amy's radar was correct. "Shirley, have I got that right?"

"Yes. You're a lucky woman, Amy."

The implication that she and Jack were together sunk in. "Oh, that…well, we aren't…" she stammered.

"You're not?" Shirley's gaze sharpened. "Oh, I'm sorry. I just assumed, after the way he looks at you…."

And just like that, Amy's pulse took that damned leap it did every time Jack's name came up. He looked at her? In what way? Amy wanted to ask but knew it would sound silly, so she schooled her features. "We're just friends." She couldn't help adding, "But you're right. He is a handsome devil. Emphasis on the devil."

She felt like she needed to put on her work hat, so she turned her full attention on the woman, reluctantly dragging it away from Jack and how he was muscling the tailgate away from the sleigh. "Are you having a good week?"

"I am. We are. It's been really relaxing, and good to get to know the new executive team better, too. We all stepped in after our takeover and it was a bit of a bumpy start. We did some teamwork stuff this morning that Jack suggested and really got to know each other better. Something to do with work and learning styles. The transition at the company has been a bit rocky. I think this is really going to help us going back." She took a deep breath. "It's so great up here, that we're talking about coming back in the summer. Doing some of the other activities not available this time of year. I think the cattle drive would be fantastic."

Shirley did not strike Amy as an outdoor girl, but there was no denying her excitement. For a moment, Amy was proud she'd been a part of the week—even if it was a small part.

"I hope you're all going to ring in the New Year with us tonight," she said sincerely.

"We wouldn't miss it," Shirley replied warmly. "I'd better go get aboard."

"Me, too." Amy followed her to the back of the sleigh, but once the other woman was aboard, Jack moved to put up the tailgate.

"You're up front with me," he said, anchoring it into place.

"I am? I don't mind sitting in the back."

"I like the company, remember? Gets lonely sitting up there all alone."

Amy doubted it. She got the feeling that Jack enjoyed his solitude in the outdoors. He was turning out to be very different from the man she expected. What was really strange was that she'd been so sure that she didn't want someone who resembled the men back home. And yet it was this Jack she really enjoyed being around. She'd been a little dazed and awestruck by the private jet and the huge house but that had worn off.

He hopped into the sleigh and then held out a hand to help her up. She put her mittened hand in his gloved one, felt his fingers tighten over hers as she stepped up. Oh, expensive trappings were all well and good. Exciting and different. But this Jack—simple, chivalrous, ordinary—was the man that made her heartbeat quicken and her eyes light up.

She wasn't sure how to even make a first move. In his own words…he wasn't interested in a relationship. He wasn't that guy.

And she wasn't, either. Except her feelings of attraction hadn't received the memo.

With a quick smile he picked up the reins and they started moving. Bells on the harness set up a jingling sound in the clear mountain air.

"Where are we headed?" she asked, taking a deep, pine-scented breath. They couldn't have asked for a more beautiful day. It was postcard-perfect.

"North and then west. The hills there are stunning and there's a little surprise waiting."

She peered up at him. His eyes sparkled at her from beneath the Stetson. "You're a great one for surprises, Jack."

"Aren't I, though?" He grinned, the reins slack in his hands, and the horses followed the invisible path beneath the snow.

"And the hat? Was that especially for today? You decided to cowboy up?"

He shrugged. "I wear it all the time in the summer. Boots, too. I told you this is a working ranch, Amy. The week of the cattle drive is insane. We have to separate the calves and the vet comes to help with the vaccinations. I leave the management of that to Miguel and Raffy—they've been doing it a lot longer than I have. But I'm in the thick of it, learning."

"And what about your business empire? Where does it fall into things?"

He shrugged. "I'm still figuring that out. I don't want to give it up entirely, but I'm not as hands-on as I used to be."

After a few moments of silence, he spoke again. "Are you disappointed? I know you said you'd had enough of those cowboy types back in Cadence Creek."

"Those cowboy types, as you put it, haven't really worked out so well for me," she answered. "And to be honest, I don't really picture myself as a ranch wife, you know? I think it was just a matter of what was available." She chuckled. "If I go away to school, I'll be meeting all sorts of people. The kind who don't wear boots and hats and walk bowlegged."

And none of those people would be Jack.

The thought bothered her more than she liked.

Chapter Nine

The sleigh ride had gone perfectly to plan, much to Jack's satisfaction. Moods were high, the weather fantastic and Raffy had ridden ahead and built a fire in the fire pit at the tiny cabin. When they arrived just before three, Raffy had cocoa steaming in a large pot on top of the iron grates. Everyone sat on the rough logs circling the fire, sipping rich cocoa and munching on Chuck's delicious shortbread cookies. After a nice break, they loaded back into the sleigh for the return journey, the conversation a little more subdued.

Amy sat next to Jack on the bench seat, her legs covered with one of the rough wool blankets to keep in the heat. As the afternoon waned, the temperature dipped, and despite any concern about appearances, Jack lifted his right arm and circled it around her, keeping her tight against his body. "It's gotten colder," he said quietly. "We should be home soon."

He drove the team easily with his left hand and was strangely gratified when her head dropped against his shoulder.

"Sorry," she murmured, barely loud enough for him to hear. "I think the cocoa's made me sleepy."

The idea of her curling up against him, soft and drowsy, caused the exact opposite reaction in him. She'd been driving him crazy all week. He hadn't expected her to end up being the sensible one and he was cursing ever saying that the ball was in her court where they were concerned. It wouldn't take much pushing to make her come around. He saw the way she looked at him. Felt the way she responded to the simplest touch.

But for some reason he felt the need to be careful. And the one thing that kept him from reneging on the agreement was knowing that he didn't want to have any regrets from these few weeks. Or rather, he didn't want *her* to have any regrets.

It also made him rather uneasy, because it was the first time in a long, long time that he'd put a woman's needs before his own.

He chanced a look down. Her eyes were closed as she dozed, her head cradled by the curve of his shoulder. So relaxed. So trusting.

He wished, for a brief moment, that she would be like this with him forever.

And that scared him to death.

They reentered the yard and he gave a nudge with his elbow, wanting to wake her before they actually stopped. "Amy," he said, trying to keep his voice low. "Amy."

Her lashes fluttered open and his heart slammed against his ribs. Her cheeks were pink from the cold and her eyes looked sleepy and sexy.

"I fell asleep."

"Yes, you did. Only for a little while. You clearly needed the rest."

"Did anyone notice?"

"I don't know. My back's been to them the whole time."

She pushed away from his shoulder. "I shouldn't have

done that. Especially after talking to one of the guests earlier..."

As they pulled up next to the barn she busied herself with folding the blanket over her lap, avoiding his eyes. He frowned. "Talking about what?"

Still she wouldn't look at him. "Oh, she just assumed that you and I were... I mean, it's easy to think that, right? We're close to the same age and all, you know..."

It seemed like every time they spoke they never quite finished a sentence. As if they were both afraid of actually saying what was riding along beneath the surface of their politeness and proper behavior.

"She thought we were lovers?"

He was gratified to see the blush flare up her cheeks. "Together," she corrected. "She thought we were a couple."

"Would that be so bad?"

He pulled up in front of the barn door. "I don't know what you mean," she answered primly. "Would it be so bad if they thought we were a couple, or would it be so bad if we actually were a couple?"

He wasn't looking for a girlfriend. So he had no idea why he answered, "Take your pick."

He hooked the reins and hopped out of the sleigh, this time not offering his hand. He moved to the back and smiled and chatted briefly as he removed the tailgate, but watched out of the corner of his eye as Amy got out and began collecting blankets.

When their guests were gone and started back to the house, Amy moved to carry the blankets into the barn. She could have just put them in the back of the sleigh, but Jack didn't bother to correct her. Instead he unhooked the team from the sleigh, led them around the side of the barn to the corral and spent a few minutes removing their harness before setting them loose in the enclosed area.

She'd be gone back to the house already. He was sure of it. But he walked the length of the barn anyway, heading for the tack room. He'd hang up the tack, take an hour of quiet to do the evening chores in Miguel's absence.

That she was in the tack room, staring up at a wall full of bridles, nearly knocked him off his pins.

After a moment's hesitation, he stepped inside. "Hey. I figured you'd be back at the house by now."

"In a bit. There's an hour or so before the supper Chuck prepared. Everyone is just relaxing for a while."

"I see." He moved to put the harness away, taking care to hang it just the way Miguel liked. Miguel kept everything in pristine shape and his pride and care showed.

"I was thinking about what you asked."

"Which question?" He put his hands on his hips as he faced her.

At least this time she met his gaze. "About if it would be so bad if people thought we were together."

Ah, so not the "if we were a couple" question. Good to know.

"And what did you come up with?"

"I don't know."

Consternation showed on her face as she looked up at him, almost as if deliberating what—or if—she should say anything more at all. In the end she let out a breath and dropped her shoulders just a bit.

"I just got to the point where I have the confidence to do something with my life that doesn't revolve around a relationship, or the hope of one. I know that's how I'm perceived and I haven't actually discouraged it. That's been my mistake. The truth is, I want to earn a spot in the world. To know I've done it myself."

"And you can't have both?"

"I don't know how. I'm barely figuring it out as it is." She gave a small, self-deprecating smile. "Jack, you've got to understand. My whole life I spent in a house with a woman who was crushed that her husband walked out on her. Whose whole existence and purpose revolved around that. I grew up thinking that being in a relationship was the only way I could be of value."

Her face changed. Her eyes widened and her lips dropped open as if she'd made a great discovery. "Holy cow," she whispered. "I just got that right now."

He'd figured her dad leaving had left its mark on her plenty. How could it not? But he hadn't considered how much she'd been affected by the parent who'd been left behind.

"You need to find your own identity," he said, nodding. He understood that. "Look, Amy. I get it. After my accident, I struggled with finding out who I really was for a long time. It wasn't a fast process."

It was unreasonable to think that Amy would have a magical shortcut to that revelation, wasn't it?

She blinked, an amazed smile touching her lips and lighting her eyes, which were far too blue in the shadowed light of the tack room.

"But still, you did figure it out, right? I spent way too much time trying to succeed where my mom had failed. And you know what? It may not even have been her failure to bear. Sure, she could have handled it better. But maybe she didn't know how. She loved him. She didn't see it coming."

He could relate. "People react in different ways when their heart gets broken," he said carefully. "And you may not know the whole story about their split."

She nodded. "She never talks about it."

"Maybe you should talk to her."

She nodded again. "Maybe. She's relied on me. I know that. I feel like going out on my own is abandoning her like he did."

"But Amy," he said, and he took a step forward, "you're not abandoning her. And part of standing on your own two feet and making decisions is dealing with personal relationships, too. It's not just about work or where you live. If you want to be there for her, you will. Whether you live twenty minutes away or twenty hours. The opposite is true, too. You could live around the corner and…" He shrugged. "Not be that close."

"Maybe. But school in Edmonton is a good place to start. A way to see beyond Cadence Creek without venturing too far. I feel like I need to be careful. Not try to jump in with both feet like I normally do."

JACK COULD FEEL her slipping away. He should probably just let it happen rather than trying to hold on to something that was steeped in futility. "I thought you said you were in a rut and didn't take risks," he said to her.

She laughed lightly. "Oh, that's true with the day-to-day stuff. Familiar surroundings breed comfort. But I spent every first date convinced that this guy was Mr. Right. And then and there…I took the plunge. No wonder I'm a joke."

"Sometimes it's not about walking away but realizing you have the strength to choose. And to own that choice. I suppose Cadence Creek isn't all bad. It has good qualities. Your family is there. Your friends are there. You might not want to cut all your ties. It doesn't have to be all or nothing." Like he'd done. Shut everyone out. Hated the world for a while.

He hadn't meant for his own bitterness to leak through

into his words. He'd meant to keep this all about Amy and what was happening between them. And still it kept coming back to Sheila, and how her weakness had caused him to lose everything.

"I don't think I'm there yet."

"I know. And part of your strength is realizing it and being honest about it. But I've got to tell you, Amy, it's been killing me. Maybe if we hadn't kissed at the wedding. Maybe if I hadn't gotten a taste of you when you first got here. But I did. And while I'm working very hard to respect your boundaries and give you the space you need, the truth is I can't get you out from under my skin."

There. He'd said it. The temperature in the room seemed to lift several degrees as her gaze clashed with his.

"You think I don't feel it?" she asked, her breath catching in her throat. "You think this has been easy for me, sticking to my guns? Me, who hasn't stuck with anything in her life up until now?"

"Maybe you haven't found the right thing to stick to," he suggested.

He took another step forward. He knew he shouldn't. But dammit, it had only been what, five days since her arrival? And he was getting impatient.

Her eyes widened. "What are you doing?"

He swallowed, knew they had to meet on equal ground. He wasn't going to be the only one pursuing. She had to choose to take a step and take this further.

"Waiting for you to meet me."

"Jack," she warned.

"You know what I want. I don't have a plan, Amy. I don't have an exit strategy or all the answers. But being this close to you is driving me crazy."

There was a long pause and he could practically hear

her considering. Then she took a hesitant step forward. "Me, too."

They were only a breath apart now. "'Me, too' what?" he asked.

Another small step. "Crazy," she whispered, and she reached up and took the Stetson off his head and dropped it to the floor. "So damn crazy." Then she raised her hands and sank them into his hair, twining the strands between her fingers while he slowly felt himself burst into flames.

He would go slowly. He would. If it killed him.

She tilted her head and stood up on tiptoe, tentatively touching her lips to his.

He responded carefully as his eyelids automatically slid closed at the first touch of her mouth. God, she tasted sweet. Like chocolate and sugar and innocence and it threatened to break the tiny thread of control he possessed. Gently she kissed him, teasing his lips, learning the shape of his mouth, exploring rather than possessing. He hadn't realized that a woman could take him apart piece by piece but that was exactly how he was feeling. As if she were stripping him bare until there was no pretense between them. The room was silent, a reverent hush surrounding his quiet undoing.

It was most unexpected, but Amy's pure and surprisingly innocent touch erased everything he'd used to build a wall around himself. His company, his success, his money, his confidence. All of it was an elaborate facade and she obliterated it like it was nothing…with one simple, sweet kiss.

Right now he was Jack. Just Jack.

His arm slid around her, pulling her close against him, ski jacket to sheepskin, and he was at once thankful and infuriated that such a thick barrier separated their bodies. And still the kiss went on, beautiful, complete.

She stepped back, and the air between them seemed tinged with regret that it had ended so soon. Her eyes were sparkling and her cheeks were blossoms of color, her lips swollen from being thoroughly kissed. Her hat sat sideways on her head, the riot of blond curls cascading beneath it and touching her shoulders. She'd never been more beautiful.

"I should get back. Everyone will be wondering where I am."

He wanted to say that she should stay. That they could find a corner of privacy in the barn and take this all the way like he was dying to do. But she deserved better. And when they made love...

Yes, he realized, it was a matter of when and not if. When they made love, he didn't want it to be a rushed affair in a cold barn on a scratchy horse blanket. She deserved soft sheets and a goose-down duvet. Soft light and all the time in the world....

He took a shaky breath.

"I'll stay and do the chores so we don't go back in together."

Her expression softened into one of gratitude. "Thank you, Jack. That's very considerate."

Considerate, hell. There was no way he could appear in front of clients right now. What they'd been up to would be painfully obvious.

But he'd allow her to think what she wanted.

"I'll see you at the party."

"Okay."

She went to move past him to the door, but he stuck out his hand and grabbed her arm, halting her progress. "Wait."

She angled her head up to look into his eyes and he searched them for a moment or two. Then he dipped his head and took her lips in one more short, sweet and wholly unsatisfactory kiss. "I'll see you later."

She didn't say a word, but he saw her throat bob as she swallowed and stepped back. He'd let her take the lead this time, but it wouldn't always be so. Not once she gave the go-ahead....

Once the barn door closed, he grabbed a shovel and threw it in the wheelbarrow. Cleaning stalls and feeding the horses would work off some of the excess energy running through his body right now.

AMY KNEW SHE should feel exhausted. The day had been long and the afternoon had ended quite unexpectedly—in Jack's arms.

She stepped carefully to the edge of the living room, which now housed the smaller table from the kitchen, laden with plates, cutlery, condiments and napkins. Along the side of the room, several waist-high occasional tables were set up, each one a different fondue station. It looked fantastic, and she worked her way around the room, lighting the fuel and adjusting the flames to heat the ingredients in the various pots.

She wasn't sure what to think about Jack. He was testing her fortitude, there was no question about that. And a lot of what he'd said made sense. It had given her a lot to think about. Possibly some of it she should regret....

Not the sleigh ride, though. She didn't regret that. How could she, when Jack had been so utterly lovely? It had been nice, sitting next to him in the front of the sleigh, his strong thigh buffeting hers as the gait of the horses rolled them along over the snow. It had been a picture-perfect afternoon...right down to the part where he'd put his arm around her and she'd curled up against his reassuring bulk. She'd closed her eyes and fantasized for a little while in the dozy space between sleep and alertness. Not that she'd ever admit that to him. Maybe Jack was right. Maybe the important thing wasn't shutting the door to the possibility of them, but exercising the right to choose what happened next.

Members of the group began arriving, so she went to the stereo and turned on the music. At the door she made sure each guest had either a sparkly tiara or a crown to add to the New Year's spirit. Later there would be party horns and a few tubes of streamers and confetti she'd discovered at a party supply store in town.

As things got under way she checked the fuel under each fondue pot and adjusted the heat. The beauty of it was people could eat as they wanted. She'd labeled fondue forks at every station with the guest's names and they mingled about, cooking beef, chicken and shrimp in hot oil or broth, dipping bread and vegetables in cheese, and her favorite: the caramel and chocolate pots where dessert waited. A tray of fruit, puffy marshmallows, pound cake cubes and cookies was waiting to tempt everyone's sweet tooth.

At the other end of the tables was the bar, set up with sparkling water, soda and wine, and two buckets where bottles of champagne were chilling for the New Year's toast.

"You really pulled off something great on short notice." Jack's voice sounded as he slid up behind her, put a hand lightly at her waist. It was a careless touch, casual, but that didn't stop the tingle from racing along her spine. After this afternoon, the light touch took on far more meaning.

"Thanks. Once I had the idea, it was just a matter of making a trip to town…."

"I've had fondue before. It's a lot of prep work. How you managed it…and the sleigh ride today, and then show up looking like you do…" His fingers gave a squeeze. "You done good, kid. Rosa couldn't have done it better. And you're far nicer to look at."

"I won't tell Miguel you said that." She couldn't help the smile that lit her face.

"Miguel would be the first to agree with me. We love Rosa to death, but you look beautiful, Amy. Really beautiful."

She'd worn the one dress she'd brought on the trip, a cobalt-blue sheath style with long sleeves and a deep neckline that merely hinted at cleavage. She'd paired it with her best shoes, too—gold sparkly heels with a platform toe. She'd longed for a chance to wear them and New Year's Eve was perfect.

Tonight, she felt like the hostess. And she was proud. Oddly enough, after this afternoon, she was doubly glad she'd brought something so flattering. She'd wanted to knock Jack's socks off after days of wearing plain jeans and sweaters.

She turned around to say thank-you and the words died on her tongue. Jack had dressed up, too—oh, not in a suit or anything, but he wore black trousers, black shoes that were so shiny she could see her reflection and a soft black button-down shirt that fit perfectly and showed off the breadth of his wide chest. It was a combination that any woman would find hard to resist.

"Wow," she breathed, looking up and meeting his eyes. "Damn, you clean up good, Mr. Shepard."

"What, these old things?" A grin crawled up his cheek. "You've seen me dressed up before. At the wedding."

"Yes, but I kind of got used to you in your jeans and plaid shirts and boots. I forgot that you…"

She broke off. She had often forgotten over the past few days that Jack was probably the richest man she'd ever met. That he didn't do chores at the barn on a regular basis, but sat in a boardroom making decisions over a wide domain.

The powerful Jack, the confidence he exuded tonight, was drop-dead gorgeous and heart-stoppingly attractive. But she was surprised to find that she preferred low-key Jack, in his worn jeans and tousled hair. In his Stetson, like today. In a sheepskin coat, with his arm around her as they kissed in the cold barn….

"You must be hungry," she said quietly, her fingers itching to touch him but she showed restraint. "You didn't come in for dinner."

"I finished up in the barn. Rosa went home from the hospital this afternoon and Miguel was under strict orders to stay away from the ranch after lunch. By the time I came in the mess was cleaned up, so I went upstairs to shower and change."

Indeed he had. He smelled good enough to eat.

"Come grab your set of fondue forks and a plate, then. As my grandma used to say, a bird can't fly on one wing. You need to eat. And let me fix you a drink. What would you like?"

"You don't need to wait on me. We're in this together, remember?"

She looked up at him and without thinking ran her tongue over her lips. "Maybe. But I can still get you a drink. You don't need to drive, so no need for tonic and lime tonight, is there?"

He reached around her for a plate and the pointed forks bundled together with his name flagged on them. "Why

Miss Wilson, are you planning on getting me drunk and taking advantage of me tonight?"

She stilled so completely that he turned his head to look over at her. Color splotched her cheeks and felt like it was burning its way down her neck at the suggestion. "Just kidding," he said.

Unsmiling, she met his gaze evenly. Heck. In for a penny, in for a pound. It was all she'd been able to think about for the past three hours, after all. "After this afternoon, the thought crossed my mind."

He nearly dropped his plate, recovering quickly but not before she saw that she'd shocked him. "Rum and cola," he requested hoarsely. "Maybe you'd better make it a double."

She walked over to the bar, conscious of the fact that his eyes were likely following her. She kept her steps slow and steady, and she wasn't above letting her hips sway gently.

She made him his cocktail and poured herself a glass of cabernet then made her way back to his side. The stereo was set to a New Year's party station and the background noise provided a little bit of cover.

He was at a fondue station, cooking a piece of chicken in hot oil. She handed him the highball glass and touched her glass to the rim. "To a successful first week, with only a few wrong turns."

"You've more than redeemed yourself for that. Everyone has had great things to say about you, Amy. You've done a very good job on very short notice."

"Thanks. It's been fun. But honestly, how Rosa manages to do this and all the cooking boggles. She must be some woman."

"She is."

"I thought I'd like to try it. I told Chuck to take tomorrow off. It's New Year's Day. He deserves the day off, don't you think?"

His chicken was done and he took it off the fork to cool, then stabbed a jumbo shrimp and stuck it in the oil. "Are you sure? Cooking for twelve can be a lot."

"It won't be Chuck's tenderloin, but I can cook. You'll see."

She wanted him to know she could do the whole job. That just because they'd had a little interlude this afternoon didn't mean she wasn't taking this opportunity seriously.

"You don't have to prove anything to me," he said quietly.

"Maybe I want to prove it to myself. Maybe I want to prove a lot of things to myself."

His gaze clung to hers. "Go for it. Far be it for me to stand in your way."

Anything else she might have said disappeared as they were joined by two of the guests, who tried their hand at the meat station. Excusing herself, Amy took a plate and dipped some veggies and crusty French bread in the sharp cheese fondue. She mingled with guests, taking the time to chat with each. Now that she didn't have to rush to the next task, she enjoyed talking to them about their hometowns and lives—places she'd never been. Maybe someday…

The evening wore on. The laughter got louder, and the CEO, who she now called Jake at his insistence, had taken over manning the bar. The fondue wound down and Amy shut off the meat and cheese stations and left the chocolate and caramel.

She was dipping a piece of Granny Smith apple in golden caramel when she sensed Jack behind her shoulder. "Little something for your sweet tooth?"

"Have you tried it yet?" she asked.

"No."

She turned around and, holding the plate to catch any syrupy drips, held the wedge of apple to his lips. "Try it."

He bit it, his firm lips closing over the fruit, his tongue sneaking out to swipe at a rebellious bit of caramel that clung to his lip.

"Delicious."

"Right? Now try this." She moved to the next pot, selected a ripe strawberry and dipped it in the dark chocolate. "Tell me this isn't heaven."

She held it up and he took it from her fingers. "Heaven," he agreed, and she grabbed another berry and swirled it through the chocolate before popping it into her mouth.

Cool sweet berry and warm rich chocolate exploded on her tongue and she closed her eyes. "Mmm."

His eyes flashed at her, telegraphing a meaning that both frightened and exhilarated her. "Good God, woman. You're going to be the death of me."

"Sorry."

"I don't think you are."

She smiled, feeling particularly saucy. "Okay, maybe I'm not, really."

"I normally enjoy my clients, but I wish they'd all disappear right about now."

"How very inhospitable of you. Why would you wish such a thing?"

He reached behind her, picked up a profiterole, touched it in the chocolate and offered it to her. She couldn't resist the soft pastry and rich cream.

"If they were gone, I'd hold you in my arms and we'd maybe dance. I'd feed you strawberries by candlelight and pour you cold champagne and keep you up half the night."

She thought she might just melt into a puddle right now. "Mr. Shepard. How brazen of you."

His teeth flashed as he smiled. "Right. Like you're not enjoying the dance we've been doing all night. I find I'm liking the new, confident Amy."

"I didn't say anything had changed."

Their gazes clung for a few more moments and then Jack checked his watch. "Only a few more minutes until midnight. I suppose we should get the champagne ready."

She let the tension between them drop, a little reluctantly, but she needed to get the confetti party poppers ready to go. "You get the champagne. I'll be right back."

She scuttled off to retrieve the bag she'd hidden behind the bar, then distributed a few of the confetti tubes to random guests. When the countdown began, she was standing a few feet away from the bar, her tube ready, a grin on her face as she watched Jack peel the foil off the first bottle of champagne.

Ten...nine...eight...

Their gazes caught and she imprinted the moment on her memory. She was here, sharing bringing in the New Year with Jack. It was a momentous feeling. She'd done it. She'd stepped outside her comfort zone and done something new and she had been good at it. At this moment she felt as if she could do anything. It would all be okay.

Five...four...three...

She put her hand on the end of the tube.

Two...one... Happy New Year!

She released the stopper on the tube and confetti and streamers popped out. Three other tubes were released at the same time, creating a festive cloud of colored paper. The loud pop of the champagne cork echoed and Amy turned her head to the sound at the same time as everyone started hugging and kissing cheeks and wishing each other a happy New Year.

Laughing, Amy went to Jack's side and reached for a pair of glasses from the polished wood countertop. He poured a little bubbly into both and put down the bottle. "Happy New Year, Amy," he said, his voice barely discernible above the party noise. "I hope it's your best year ever."

"Happy New Year, Jack." She touched the rim of her glass to his and they drank, their gazes locked. The champagne was dry and fizzy, the tart taste lingering on her tongue. She lowered her glass. He lowered his. And it seemed the most natural thing in the world for him to step forward and kiss her—the traditional celebration of ringing in a new year.

Her lashes fluttered closed as awareness zinged through her body. His lips were soft, inviting and, perhaps best—and worst—of all, familiar.

She stepped back first, aware that they were in front of guests. She pasted on a smile and said, "Happy New Year!" perhaps a little too brightly. With her heart pounding, she turned to the nearest guest and offered a friendly hug and New Year's wish, determined to mix with the group until things wound down.

There'd be time later to sort out what was happening. In private. Because tonight Amy had finally made up her mind what she wanted. And she was going to go after it.

Chapter Ten

The last straggler had wandered off to bed and Amy had packaged up the leftover food and put it in the fridge. The dishwasher was stacked and running, and the clock on the microwave read 1:17 a.m.

She should have been exhausted. Should have been ready to take off her shoes and climb into her comfy bed and fall into a deep, satisfying sleep.

Instead she made her way upstairs, down the long hallway past the guest rooms, to the door on the right that was the master bedroom. Jack's. She carried a small tray containing the last of the champagne, as well as a small bowl of strawberries and a dish of chocolate. That and her bravery, which she hoped wasn't going to desert her at the last minute.

She tapped lightly on the door.

Muffled footsteps approached and she held her breath as the knob turned. The door opened, revealing Jack in the breach. He'd removed his shoes and shirt but still wore his trousers. It was the first time she'd seen him without a shirt on and her mouth went dry.

He might be a former athlete but there was nothing former about the breadth of his chest and shoulders, or the rippled six-pack. He'd definitely kept himself in shape.

He looked at her, down at the tray, and wordlessly

stepped back, opening the door for her to come in. He closed it behind her, sealing them in a cocoon of privacy and possibility.

"A private celebration?" he asked quietly, as she put the tray down onto a side table.

She didn't know how to respond, so she merely poured two glasses of champagne and handed one to him. Then she took a strawberry, dipped it in chocolate and lifted it to his lips. This was what he'd articulated earlier. Her, champagne, strawberries and chocolate and privacy....

He took it from her fingers, then without taking his eyes off her, reached out and found another berry. This time he fed her, and they both took a drink.

By the time they'd eaten another two berries, the air in the room had reached a fever pitch, thick with anticipation. Jack drained the last of his champagne, his eyes dark with intent. She finished hers and he took the glass from her fingers, putting them both on the table.

He framed her face with his hands and drew her in for a long, dark kiss. Different from any of the ones that had come before. This time it was full of intent, ripe with the knowledge that tonight neither of them was planning on walking away. It was a promise of things to come, an electrifying harbinger of the pleasure waiting for them both. She hoped... A butterfly flutter of doubt winged its way through her stomach, as she wondered if she could possibly be enough woman for a man like Jack. But then she pushed the thought aside. The one conclusion she'd come to for sure was that if she didn't do this she'd never know and she'd regret it for as long as she lived.

He reached for the tie of her wraparound dress and she felt the fabric fall away. Nerves fizzed all over her body and it was hard to breathe as he gently pushed the dress off her shoulders and it slid to the floor. She was standing there wearing nothing more than her lace bra and panties and her sparkly gold shoes. Jack's eyes glowed at her and his lips curved ever so slightly. "You're beautiful," he murmured, reaching out and running a finger over the skin of her shoulder. "More beautiful than I imagined."

"Jack…"

"Shh," he said, and the way he was stroking her skin nearly had her purring. "We'll go slow. Promise."

To prove his point, he kissed her again, taking his time, letting her get used to the feel of his hands on her skin. His chest was warm and firm pressed against hers. Finally, when her knees got weak, he took her hand and led her to his bed.

"You're sure?" he asked, and she loved how his gaze was hungry and yet serious. It made her feel both desirable and respected, something she hadn't expected. She wanted to be with him. Had from the very first night. She had no expectations, was under no illusions. There was just the here and now.

This was her moment to be brave. To take a chance.

"I'm sure," she whispered, nodding. "Very, very sure."

The only light in the room was the bedside lamp, casting a soft glow over the bed. Amy bit down on her lip. With the light on he would see everything. She would see everything…and yet asking to turn the light off seemed silly.

He must have followed the direction of her gaze because he looked back at her and smiled. "Do you want it off?"

"Maybe…no…whatever you want."

She sounded pathetic. He was going to regret this. What if he backed away, changed his mind?

Instead he merely reached over and pushed the switch, casting the room into darkness.

"Come here," he said, and she swore she could hear her own heartbeat as she kneeled on the soft duvet.

He took her in his arms and the rest of her fears disappeared. There was no room for misgivings. There was just room for her to feel as he let his weight press her down into the mattress. She'd been wrong about the light. In the darkness all her other senses sharpened so that she felt every soft touch, heard every aroused breath as their limbs twined together. As her eyes adjusted, she became aware of the shadow of him, how his hair appeared darker than his skin, how his eyes still managed to glow at her with a black intensity that turned her bones to jelly. At some point his pants came off and hit the floor with a jangle of his belt buckle; shortly after, her underwear followed and she wondered how it was possible to feel this good.

He reached into the bedside table for a condom and she knew this was her last moment to turn back. That if she said stop, he would. Without a doubt. Because Jack was possibly the most honorable, honest man she'd ever met.

But she said nothing. And when he came back to her, she lifted her arms in welcome.

SUNLIGHT FILTERED THROUGH the blinds and Amy squinted as she woke. Beside her, Jack breathed deeply, still asleep. She shifted slightly, careful not to wake him. A quick adjustment of the sheets revealed what she'd guessed…. He was completely naked. And beautiful.

Tears stung her eyes and she blinked them away. It would be terribly easy to love him—if she allowed herself to. He'd been so careful. So thorough, so loving. The perfect lover to make her feel cherished and valued. Gentle yet powerful. For a few magical moments, the noise of life had faded away and it had just been the two of them. No, not even the two of them. They'd been one. One heartbeat, one body, one soul. She'd felt it. Right in the moment before she'd come apart in his arms.

The memory made her blush, so she carefully slid out from under the sheets and tiptoed around the bed until she found her underwear and dress. Jack was still sleeping soundly, and she regretted having to leave, but there were ten other people in the house who were expecting breakfast. Ten other people who were not expecting her to tiptoe out of Jack's room and do the walk of shame through the house.

With one last look of longing at his slumbering form, she gathered up her shoes. She soundlessly turned the doorknob and slipped out, closing it quietly behind her as she made a quick, fleet-footed trip down the hall to the room that was hers. A check of her watch told her she only had maybe five minutes to shower, so she immediately shed her clothes and stepped under the hot spray. Her hair was wet and she didn't bother with makeup before heading for the kitchen. There'd be time for that later....

She had bacon frying and was dipping bread for French toast when she heard a sound in the doorway. Jack. Dressed in jeans and a plaid shirt left untucked, his hair damp and tousled as if he'd just run his hands through it after his shower. Her tongue felt thick and stuck to the roof of her mouth as their eyes met.

"Good morning," he said quietly, and then he came forward and kissed her lightly on the temple. "Smells good in here."

She tried to collect her thoughts, focused on putting the soggy bread on the electric skillet to fry. "Good morning."

"You snuck out without waking me."

"You were sleeping like a log."

He chuckled. "I've always wondered where that saying came from. How do logs sleep, anyway?"

"Unmoving, I would suppose," she answered, and couldn't help the tiny smile on her lips. "I didn't want to be late getting breakfast, and it's already going on nine."

"Late night last night and everyone's sleeping in."

"So it would seem."

"Can I help?"

She wasn't sure if she were relieved or disappointed that they weren't going to talk about what had happened. On one hand, talking would probably muddy the waters. Take them into territory neither of them wanted to explore. On the other hand, though, saying nothing made it feel like they were ignoring it. Like it had meant... nothing.

Hell.

"Do you know how to make coffee? Not one cup at a time, but in the regular machine?"

"I think I can handle that."

She turned the first pieces of French toast, then flipped the bacon. As the coffee started to perk, she put the finished pieces and slices in the warming oven. Another pan of bacon was set to fry, new bread was put on the skillet and she started cracking eggs into a bowl. She'd scramble those just before it was time to serve the meal so they wouldn't be dry.

When things were cooking just right, she fixed a tray of butter, syrup and berries to go with the French toast and delivered it to the dining room. To her surprise, Jack followed with plates, then forks, knives, spoons and juice glasses. "Thanks," she said, darting back to the kitchen.

She was taking the next batch of toast off the skillet when Jack placed a cup of coffee by her elbow.

It all felt so…normal. She frowned. She couldn't let it be that way. Couldn't let herself be seduced by any ideas that had no bearing on reality.

"Cream and two sugars, right?"

She nodded. "Yeah. Thanks."

He knew how she took her coffee.

"Jack, about last night…"

He came up behind her and put a hand on her waist. "You're not having morning-after regrets, are you?"

Her muscles tensed and she forced herself to relax and keep her voice casual. "Are you?"

He kissed the small bit of skin between the collar of her T-shirt and her neck. "Of course not."

"Oh." Delight skittered down her arms at the simple kiss. "Me, either."

"But I'm thinking you'll be more comfortable if we're discreet around the guests," he said, going back to the coffeemaker and pouring his own cup of coffee.

"Yes, I would. Doing my job and…us—" she struggled around the word "—should be separate."

"I agree completely."

That was it? No argument? No innuendos? Was it really just that simple for him? Because she was having a hard time breathing simply from having him in the same room. It wasn't going to be particularly easy for her to be discreet. She'd have to work on a poker face. But apparently for Jack—no problem.

That he'd find it so easy was slightly annoying.

She heard footsteps out in the main area of the house, and the sound of muffled voices, meaning their time to chat was cut short. The group was up and would be expecting breakfast straightaway. She flipped the last pieces of toast and gave Jack a bright, if somewhat false, smile.

"Could you get everyone started with coffee, and then come back and put on a fresh pot?"

"Sure."

"And click the button on the kettle, so I can make a pot of tea," she added. Emotions churning, she put butter in a fry pan and grabbed the bowl of eggs.

When he returned, she'd put the French toast on a pretty platter, had another rectangular plate piled with crisp bacon and was scooping scrambled eggs into a bowl. "We're ready," she said, a little nervous about her first time cooking for the group. Still, she'd kept it pretty simple.

He took the French toast while she followed with the bacon and eggs. And then they proceeded to eat breakfast and chat around the table as if last night never happened.

That afternoon was the first time that the guests split into two groups for different activities. The men had chosen a three-hour snowmobile tour at a nearby resort, and the women had unilaterally gone for a spa afternoon complete with facials, pedicures and massages.

Amy had just finished the housekeeping and was stirring the massive Crock-Pot of pasta sauce when Jack stuck his head into the kitchen. "You nearly ready?" he asked.

"Ready? Is it time to go already?" She checked her watch. Where had the day gone? She hadn't stopped since getting up this morning, but she was planning an hour or so of downtime this afternoon when she had the ranch house to herself.

"The group is booked in for two o'clock. The confirmation just came to the email this morning. Your first appointment is a facial. Are you looking forward to it?"

A facial? Her? "Wait, I'm not part of the group. Aren't I just doing drop-off and pickup?"

He grinned. "I called and added you in. Figured you deserved a spa day same as anyone else."

She wasn't sure if she should be pleased or not, though she was leaning toward pleased because an afternoon at a spa sounded heavenly and it was something she'd never been able to afford. "But Jack, it's expensive...."

"Must I remind you that I'm not paying you a wage this week? Consider it a well-earned perk."

Ah. It was all about business, then; not a lover's gift. She was disappointed somehow. They hadn't had a moment to talk since breakfast. No stolen seconds to sneak a kiss. For heaven's sake, it was like he wasn't affected at all! Like nothing monumental had happened between them.

She took a breath and reminded herself that Jack was probably used to this sort of affair. He certainly seemed confident enough about it. She was the one wigging out. And he was right. She'd worked her butt off and the agreement was that she'd take advantage of activities during her stay. "Are you sure?" she asked.

"It's done. I logged on and looked after what email came in this morning since you were so busy."

Which she would have looked after this afternoon—when she had time to breathe.

"Let me get my things, then. Goodness, I'm glad I planned spaghetti for dinner."

"I'm off with the boys, snowmobiling. Have fun, okay? I'll see you later."

He was gone.

She felt oddly deflated. Yesterday every touch, every exchange, had felt personal. Like a lead-up to something. There was subtext—from how they looked at each other to the words they said and the simplest touch. Today it was like she'd imagined it all. Maybe Jack had achieved his objective and that was enough. He had already moved on and lost interest.

She didn't want to believe it, but how else could she explain his detached behavior today? It was almost as if that brief little shoulder kiss hadn't happened. Or that it was his way of letting her down easy. A few token gestures as he put distance between them.

She should have known better. She did know better. And once more she'd let her emotions take over. Because despite telling herself over and over that she understood the limitations of their relationship, it had only taken one night to put her on an irreversible course.

She'd fallen for Jack Shepard.

JACK LET OUT a deep breath as he stood on the front step. For some reason he didn't want to go inside. To say he was freaking out would be an understatement.

Oh, he'd covered his tracks all right this morning. A platonic kiss on the temple, that little one on her shoulder… It had appeased her without being too much. And booking her in for the spa afternoon had been a great idea.

But now she was waiting inside. The group was in there, getting ready for dinner. And things had changed between them. He couldn't deny that. He'd stupidly believed that they could be intimate with each other and be sensible since they both knew what was what.

What an idiot he'd been. Sex always changed things. He'd let his libido take over instead of his common sense. Something he hadn't done in a very long time.

He couldn't stand in the cold forever, so he turned the knob and went inside, taking a deep breath and preparing himself to be "on" as host. They still had to get through tonight and tomorrow morning. And the longer he could put off a conversation, the better. He had no idea what he was going to say.

Music was playing on the stereo and a fire crackled merrily in the fireplace. He took off his coat and boots and put them away, then made his way through to where the noise was coming from. He found Amy in the kitchen, a couple of the women of the group with her. All three had glasses of wine on the go. As Amy added pasta to a huge pot, another woman chopped vegetables for salad and the third was putting grated cheese on four long garlic bread halves.

"Hey, you're back." Amy noticed him there and he smiled. He could do this. They'd talk later, but for now nothing had changed. His pulse beat a warning at his throat.... The urge to back away warred with his very real desire for her. That was what scared him most. That he couldn't seem to put her out of his mind, put their relationship in perspective. She'd awakened some dormant need in him that he really never wanted to feel again. He liked her. He was attracted to her. But it stopped there. Didn't it?

"Yeah. The trails were great. We stayed out a bit longer than we planned."

The woman he recognized as Mandy spoke up. "We sent the boys to get washed up for dinner. It won't be long."

"I see you recruited help," he said, trying to relax his cheeks as he smiled so it wouldn't look forced.

Amy shrugged. "We got talking on the way back from the spa. It's been fun."

"Amy was telling us all about you, Jack."

His ears suddenly started to get warm. "Me?" The word sounded strangled. What happened to discreet?

Amy's eyes twinkled at him. "I was telling them about your brother's wedding and how you came into the women's bathroom."

"Oh, that." Relief sluiced through him.

"It was very gallant of you, Jack." The other woman—he thought her name was Shirley—jumped into the conversation. "And then you danced with her. Jack Shepard to the rescue."

He felt as if he were choking. "It wasn't that big of a deal, really."

Amy took the tray of garlic bread and slid it into the oven. "Well, it saved my pride."

Mandy scraped diced cucumber into the salad bowl. "How did you end up here, Amy?"

He watched as Amy straightened, met his gaze briefly and then turned away. "Jack's regular coordinator was in an accident. I'm going to be studying hospitality management in the fall. I offered to come down and help him out for a few weeks."

"So it's just business? Even after that romantic wedding dance?"

He met Amy's gaze again. Boy, wasn't he in a hard place now. If he said no, it meant there was definitely something between them. That it was personal. Which of course it was, but he wasn't anywhere close to being comfortable with it. And if he said yes, it was basically telling Amy that last night didn't matter.

He could at least explain to her later, couldn't he? Surely she'd understand. She'd been very conscious about what the guests thought all week.

"Just business," he confirmed. "Amy's been a lifesaver during your visit. I couldn't have run this week without her."

He couldn't look at her face, but he saw out of the corner of his eye how she turned back to the stove and stirred the pasta.

"Excuse me, ladies. I'd better go wash up for dinner."

He nodded and slipped from the room, a sense of dread settling heavily in his stomach. What he was feeling for Amy couldn't be love. He knew that. And he hadn't wanted to hurt her feelings.

But it was clear he'd been fooling himself into believing she was like the other women he'd dated over the years. None of them had been serious. All of them had known he wasn't in the market for anything permanent and at the end they'd parted amicably. It had all been very civilized.

He'd thought it could be the same with Amy. And it wasn't. She wasn't a casual-affair kind of girl, was she? He'd known that from the start and had ignored it. Now he'd have to find a way to let her down gently.

One thing was for sure. He wasn't going to tackle that mountain until his clients were on their way back to California and the house was their own. If a private conversation was going to go badly, he preferred that his business wasn't brought into it.

Chapter Eleven

Once the van and SUV had pulled away, Amy let the smile she'd been holding for what felt like hours slip away from her lips.

Maybe she should forget all about working in the hospitality field and go into acting. Because she'd sure done a lot of that over the past twenty-four hours.

She let out a big breath and turned away from the window, then headed upstairs to the guest rooms, where she began viciously stripping sheets from the beds. In no time she had the first load of bedding in the washer and she had a load of towels ready to go next. Then she set about dusting and vacuuming each room, and scoured the bathrooms from top to bottom. By the time Jack was back from the airport, she'd stripped down to a T-shirt and her hair was coming out of her ponytail in little wisps as the exertion of the morning's tasks worked out her frustrations and she tried to make sense of her feelings. All she came up with was that she was mad. Mad at Jack for pushing her aside. And mad at herself for not foreseeing this would happen.

"Wow. You've whipped through here like a tornado." Jack's rich voice came across the room as she switched sheets over into the dryer.

"It needed to be done, and the house was quiet."

She straightened, put her hands on her lower back and stretched. Did he have to sound so damned cheerful? "It seems quiet with everyone gone."

"Just you and me," he said, and silence stretched out uncomfortably between them.

She set the timer and hit the button. She'd had all morning to think and wonder. Wonder why Jack had conveniently stayed up late talking with guests last night. Why he'd offered a bland "good night" when she'd finally announced she was going off to bed. He hadn't kissed her, hadn't given her the least bit of encouragement that they were okay. She wasn't stupid. She knew regret and withdrawal when she saw it. She'd seen it enough times, after all.

"Yeah. Just you and me. Nowhere for you really to hide now, is there?"

She faced him evenly. The old Amy would have smiled and tried to make nice. Would have turned on the charm. Might have been a bit needy, too. But being away—even such a short time—had changed her. There was no one else around to remind her of old patterns. No one to think "how typically Amy" except for the voice whispering in her own ear. And she was getting better at telling that voice to be quiet. She was done settling for scraps. And scraps were all Jack had given her in the end.

And then there was Jack himself. On that first strange and magical night at the wedding, he'd said something to her. Something about doing better than Rhys because she deserved someone who wanted to be with her. Only with her. Who couldn't go on another day without her. And he had been right.

In the close quarters of the past week, in the intimate moments and because of the undeniable attraction, she'd let herself forget that. But she remembered now. And the truth was, she did have regrets.

She sighed, looking into his ever-so-handsome face. Jack was gorgeous. Rich. Successful. Funny. And for the first time in her life she realized she deserved better.

He frowned at her. "Who's hiding?"

He wasn't going to make this conversation easy, was he? She was going to have to ask. And it was humiliating. It reminded her of all the times she'd been pushed aside and she'd pathetically wondered what was wrong with her—frequently out loud.

She moved past him and into the main working area of the kitchen. "Look, Jack. I promised myself that no matter what happened between us I wasn't going to be needy or clingy. So I'm not. Your actions yesterday spoke loudly enough."

She heard him sigh heavily. "I knew deep down that if we did this, it would become a *thing*."

Her temper flared just a bit at his dismissive tone. "A *thing?* Wow, Jack. I told you that I understood your position on a relationship. You think I went to your room the other night under some delusion that this was more than it is?"

"Did you?"

She stopped and thought about it for a moment. Knew that the best way to say what she had to say was face-to-face so she turned to him, even though she could feel her cheeks flame. "No, I didn't. I wanted you. We've both been very clear about what we want and more importantly what we don't want. You don't want a relationship. I don't want to get derailed from my plans. Give me a little credit, please."

She tried very hard to ignore the little swirl of guilt that said she was at least *partially* lying. She hadn't gone to his room with any delusions. But she'd left his room in a very different state of mind.

"Things change when people become...intimate."

"Did I lead you to believe anything had changed?"

There was a beat of silence. "No, you didn't."

The stupid thing was, it had changed. In the moment they'd come together something had shifted inside her. Clicked into place. Like she was meant to be in this moment with this particular man. That it was perfect. That he was perfect.

She'd been looking for that feeling of rightness for such a long time. And when it came, it had scared the crap out of her. Because it wasn't—couldn't be—real. Not with Jack.

But at least she'd been willing to enjoy whatever was between them for the duration. Leaving Jack would be hard but she knew it was how it had to be and she'd accepted that.

But Jack...he'd withdrawn. That was what really hurt.

She lifted her eyes and met his. "Were you disappointed? Is that it?"

"Disappointed?" His eyes flashed, the first real sign of emotion she'd seen from him in over twenty-four hours. "You think I am disappointed in what happened?" He took a step toward her. "In you?"

"Why else would you withdraw? Make things so... cool between us? I've seen the brush-off, Jack. I'm well versed in it. Yours was classic. Just enough contact to keep things from blowing up. A little kiss. A smile. A nice gesture, like the spa. But definitely keeping your distance. I'm not stupid, Jack. There were opportunities if you'd wanted to take advantage of them."

For the first time she could remember, Jack blushed. He cleared his throat roughly. "I was not disappointed.

Not in that night. Definitely not in you. Let's get that straight right from the beginning."

The words sent a shaft of heat rushing through her. If he wasn't disappointed, then what?

An alternative popped into her mind but she brushed it away. No, it wasn't possible. Jack must be worried about her feeling too much for him, not the other way around. He wasn't that guy. He was older, more experienced and very, very sure of himself. The idea that "things changed" for Jack because of one night of sex was impossible.

"Then why did you back away?"

His gaze shifted to the side. "We did still have guests in the house. Ones you said had already speculated about us. I didn't want to give them any confirmation of that. It's a professional business."

He was parroting her own excuse back to her. Clever. Or not. Because he'd seen fit to put his arm around her on the sleigh, to go on an intimate dogsled ride for two, to flirt openly and kiss her in front of everyone on New Year's Eve.

He was covering. Why else would he look away?

Softly, very softly, she said, "You're lying. I don't know why, but you are."

She turned and left the kitchen, her heart thrumming against the wall of her chest. Where had this confident woman come from? Maybe she'd been inside all along. Amy rather suspected that she'd hid this side of herself behind the good-time facade because she was afraid of showing her true self to anyone. Afraid of being vulnerable enough to let anyone really hurt her. Because the truth was, despite all the failed relationship attempts, two men had come close to breaking her heart years ago. Her father when he walked out. And Terry when he'd walked away as if she'd meant nothing. She really hadn't let anyone else in since.

Until Jack. And she was all right there because they'd already laid out the ground rules. Or that had been the plan, anyway. Boom.

She was nearly to the stairs when Jack said her name. "Amy. Wait."

"Wait for what?" She turned with her hand on the banister. "Now that everyone's gone you're going to whisk me away for an hour of bliss?"

Problem with that was, it actually sounded quite heavenly....

"That wasn't what I was going to say."

"I know. Just the same as I know your guest excuse is bogus. Because we had guests the night before. If you'd wanted to be with me, you would have gone to bed instead of staying up. You would have found a moment to tell me to meet you in your room, or you would have come to mine, or you would have found a window of opportunity to steal a kiss and make a plan. You didn't."

She began walking up the stairs.

"Where are you going?"

The answer was instantly clear to her, and came as quite a surprise considering the pains she'd taken to get away from home. "You've got another couple of days before the next group comes in. Chuck's staying on to cook and the bookwork is pretty much caught up. I'm sure you can find someone to change the sheets and launder the towels for a few days. I'd like to go back to Cadence Creek."

She got one good look at his gaping mouth and felt guilty...and perhaps a bit dramatic. But she was done with begging, done with wasting her time with men who didn't think she was good enough.

Especially with men who had the power to hurt her. And Jack did. More than he possibly knew. And she never wanted him to know that painful truth.

JACK STOOD LOOKING up the stairs. He could hear Amy's feet on the floor above him, moving about her bedroom. Was she packing? What the hell had just happened?

She was mad at him. He got that. He even deserved it. And she'd seen right through his excuse, dammit. For a girl who gave the impression of not being especially bright, she was sharp as a tack. She'd whipped his office into shape in record time. Been fantastic at the job he'd given her. And now she was being all insightful.

That was what scared him most. That she might see the truth. He couldn't even really admit it to himself, so he'd be damned if he could admit it to anyone else.

His stomach twisted into knots. He had to talk to her but had no idea what to say.

He climbed the stairs, each step heavy. For a second he contemplated just driving her to the airport and putting her on a plane back to Edmonton. He knew if he called Callum or Avery one of them would pick her up.

But that would be a coward's way out. Jack didn't much like being considered a coward. Never had.

He knocked on the door to her room before pushing it open.

She was packing. Neatly folding her clothes into the one suitcase she'd brought. She was right. He'd treated her badly. Definitely given her the cold shoulder after pursuing her all week. All because she'd made him feel things he'd never thought to feel again.

"You don't have to go."

"I want to."

Her voice was firm and her decisiveness stung. "I

have to go to Vancouver for a few days. You could have the place to yourself. If you don't want to work the next group, I can hire someone. But you're welcome to stay."

Her lips thinned. He'd said the wrong thing, hadn't he?

"What's the point in me staying? I might as well go back, see if Melissa has any shifts for me. It's just going to be awkward, Jack. Like I knew it would be. It's better if I go. We're just prolonging the inevitable."

"You regret what happened between us?" Somehow the question left him feeling hollow.

Her hands paused over a sweater, then she smoothed it on the pile of clothes in the case. "I didn't say that."

"Then…"

She didn't let him finish. "I regret that it got weird. Like you said—things change when people become intimate. I should have known better."

It grated that she was putting it all on herself, when it wasn't her fault. Grated further that it meant he had to fess up that he was to blame. "It's going to sound lame if I say it's me, not you," he said. "But it is. You didn't do anything wrong, Amy."

"That's good to know."

Damn, she wasn't going to let him off the hook. "That's all you have to say?"

She turned then. He wasn't sure if her eyes were so bright because she was angry or if she'd been fighting tears. But the blue depths bit into him. He hadn't meant to hurt her, and he had.

"I've told you a lot of my history. I'm done with begging, Jack. Or asking for second chances to do better. It's not who I want to be. I'm not desperate."

"I never said you were desperate."

"No," she answered, with a little nod. "I did. I've been my own worst enemy for a long time. Begging for scraps of affection and attention, wanting someone to think I was good enough. And I think I kept trying because I needed to redeem myself. It wasn't just you at the wedding, though that helped open my eyes. It was Christmas, and seeing my mom still looking so miserable. The power to change was always there in her reach and she never grabbed it. I don't want to be that way. If I don't stand my ground this time, it will be all too easy to go back to old patterns. Like it or not, Jack, you're my stand."

"So you're really going."

"You don't love me, Jack. It was a great night but it scared you for some reason. Scared you enough you backed off in a major hurry."

"I just need some time…"

"Time won't change anything for you. And I'm starting to realize that I have enough to fix about myself that I can't start trying to fix you, too."

Shit. He hated that she was right. But then, from the beginning he'd sensed she was far more intuitive than she was ever given credit for. Like that night at the wedding. She hadn't been looking to score with Rhys. She'd been matchmaking, trying to push Rhys and Taylor together. Even his parents liked her. His mother had called her "smart as a whip and not afraid of hard work."

Who was he to mess up her plans? In her words, all it would do was prolong the inevitable.

"If you need a reference for school or for any sort of job, you let me know, okay?"

She smiled but it didn't reach her eyes. "Thanks."

She turned back to her packing.

Something didn't feel right. He frowned, stayed in the doorway, not wanting to leave just yet. "Amy, I really am sorry about yesterday. I know I pushed for things to move ahead between us. I thought we…thought I…could handle it, no problem. It's never been a problem before…."

Didn't *that* make him sound great?

She put the cover over the suitcase and zipped it up. "Why is it this time, do you think?"

He went to her side and lifted the case off the bed and put it on the floor. "I don't know." He reached out and gripped her hand. "Amy…"

For a long moment they both stared at their joined hands. Jack felt like his breath was strangling in his chest. Her fingers were so soft, resting in his palm. When he looked up, she was watching him with sadness in her eyes. And perhaps a lot more understanding than he was comfortable with.

"You do know," she accused gently. "But you're not ready to deal with it." She withdrew her hand from his. "I just need to go, Jack. I hope you understand."

"I do. And I'm sorry."

"I know you are."

"Let me know when you're ready. I'll look at getting you a flight."

"Thanks."

He left the room. Thanks, hell. After years of being calm, focused, detached…he was suddenly none of those things. She'd swooped in without trying and turned everything on its head. He was a man who always stayed in control. Who enjoyed taking risks, but when it came to interpersonal decisions, practical clarity was his specialty. It had made him stupidly successful.

He should be the one handling this situation. Instead it was Amy who was being strong and smart and sure of herself. Who was able to think logically. Who saw yesterday for what it was: panic.

And who, he realized, had decided it wasn't worth hanging around for. That fixing him was too much trouble.

Intellectually he knew that no one could fix what was wrong with him but himself. But on another level, he was hurt that once again, someone thought he wasn't even worth the effort.

AMY EXPECTED TO fly back commercial—take a puddle jumper somewhere bigger and then a flight to Edmonton. But when she and Jack got to the airport, the same private jet was waiting to take her home.

"Jack," she said, embarrassed now that she'd been so short with him earlier. So blunt: "You didn't have to do this."

He shrugged. "I'd booked it for tomorrow morning anyway, for my Vancouver trip. The pilot will take you to Edmonton and then come back here for the night. Don't worry."

For a brief moment she'd felt special. Felt like maybe there was a bit of hope they could patch things together and at least get back to being comfortable with each other. But he made it sound like it had been no effort at all to arrange her transportation. It took some of the thrill out of it.

"Right."

She stopped and held out her hand for her suitcase, which he'd been rolling behind him. Her carry-on rested heavily on her shoulder. "I've got to go through the security check before I get on," she said.

"I know."

But he didn't hand over her bag right away. Instead he stood there, in that damned sheepskin jacket, his hair windblown by the winter breeze and cheeks ruddy from walking from the car to the terminal.

"Jack," she said quietly.

"You're sure you have to go?"

He was going to draw it out longer. Test her fortitude. He probably had no idea how hard it was to leave,
or how close she was to saying no. The only thing keeping her from staying was knowing that nothing would
change in another week—except that she might be even
more hurt in the end. Because Jack, for all his charm and
flirting, was not about to open his heart. He'd closed it
years ago when Sheila had betrayed him. Locked it up
and thrown away the key. It didn't take a rocket scientist
to figure that out.

And what he didn't know was how close she was to
falling for him. All the way. Her heart was already fully
involved. Thankfully her head hadn't abandoned her yet.
She'd known from the start that Jack wasn't the guy for
her. It was the only thing holding her back from tumbling all the way in.

"I should go."

"The pilot will wait if I tell him to wait. He's on my
dime," Jack said irritably.

She smiled a little. "Ah, there he is. The boss who is
used to having his orders obeyed. He'd kind of disappeared for a while."

"He did?"

"You're always charming, Jack. But you're less…
autocratic at the ranch." She tilted her head. "Which
one's the real you?"

His gaze caught hers, terribly complicated and uncer-
tain. At least she wasn't easy to walk away from. It made
her feel a teensy bit better.

"I'd better go," she repeated.

Jack let go of the handle of her suitcase, but instead of

handing it to her, he took a step and closed the gap between them. His hands cradled her face and she gasped in a small breath in the heartbeat before his lips came crashing down on hers.

Her carry-on slipped from her shoulder and dropped to the floor, but Amy barely heard the thump. This was the Jack she remembered, the Jack she'd been so tempted by in the tack room and again in his room. Passionate, open, without the walls he kept around himself. He made a small sound in his throat as the kiss went deeper and Amy was vaguely aware that they were in public and there was the sound of voices around them but she didn't pull away. Not if this were the last time.

Finally, the words *get a room* sunk into her consciousness and she closed her lips, stopping the kiss. She could still taste him, still feel him there. Could still feel the press of his fingers into her arms, the way his body fit against hers. She had to leave, right now. Because if she said anything it would be to express how she truly felt and it was the last thing Jack wanted to hear.

It would send him running in the other direction even faster than making love had.

Without meeting his eyes she picked up her carry-on, grabbed the handle of her suitcase in a death grip and began wheeling her way to the security check. She didn't look back, though she was tempted. Instead she met the pilot with a smile, walked out to the plane, climbed the steps and settled into the leather seat.

As they taxied past the small airport, she chanced a look at the windows facing the runway. And imagined, just for a flash, that Jack was still standing there watching her leave. But when they were airborne she looked down at the parking lot and saw that his SUV was gone from the spot where he'd parked it.

She was going home. To start over.

Funny how the idea sounded heartily depressing.

Chapter Twelve

Cadence Creek was in the full throes of winter when Amy returned from Montana. An Arctic front had pushed south, cloaking the area in terribly frigid temperatures. On her first week back, school was canceled twice because of the wind chill. She went back to work at the flower shop, but business was slow. Still, it surprised her to find she was happy to be home. It was familiar. And as Jack had said—it wasn't all bad.

Jack.

She hadn't heard from him since that day at the airport. Why she thought she would, she didn't quite know. It had been fairly final, after all, and there was no reason for the phone to ring. None at all. Except…

Except she couldn't quite shake the feeling that things had been left unsaid.

Amy rang off the cash register at the end of her shift, turned over the closed sign on the door and went to the office to count out the deposit and make sure the float for the next day was ready. Foothills Floral was quiet and peaceful as she wrote up the deposit slip. It was dark outside when she closed the door behind her, carrying the deposit in her purse. A block away was the bank and she dropped the deposit into the after-hours slot.

The pace sure was slower than Aspen Valley. Not that

doing laundry and making beds was her idea of fun, but
the variety of tasks and people suited her. She'd enjoyed
her time there despite how it had ended. And now that
she was home, she was looking forward to the fall se-
mester and going to school.

She could be good at this. If nothing else, the week
working at Jack's had shown her that her instincts were
right. She was efficient and good with people. More-
over, she liked making them feel at home. She'd never
considered herself a nurturer, but there was no denying
that she'd found a certain satisfaction with that compo-
nent of the job at Jack's.

When she arrived at home, her mom had supper ready.
Amy had started looking at Mary differently since coming back. How it must have hurt to have her husband
just walk out like that. In all the time Amy had wished
her mom would just get over it and move on, she hadn't
considered love and what the loss of that love might do
to a person.

She suspected Jack had loved Sheila that way. And
while Amy's mom had hidden herself away, working as
a data clerk in a cubicle where she could be anonymous
and coming home to an empty house, Jack had gone the
other way—he lived every moment out loud. People dealt
with things in different ways. Falling for Jack had made
her look at the people around her a little differently, and
that wasn't a bad thing.

"Mom?" Amy walked into the small kitchen and saw
her mom draining potatoes at the sink. "Hey. You made
roast beef? Yum." The scent of the roast was thick in the
air. Amy's stomach rumbled.

"It's good to have you home to cook for," Mary said,
taking the lid off the potatoes so that steam billowed up.

Amy frowned, considering her mother's words, and

voiced something that had been bothering her for the past few weeks. "Mom, what are you going to do when I go away to school?"

Mary avoided her eyes. "Manage. Always figured you'd leave at some point."

"I'm worried you'll be lonely."

Mary paused with the potato masher in her hand and looked up at Amy. "Honey, I've been lonely for over fifteen years. I'm happy you're going to do something outside of Cadence Creek. You…" Her voice thickened and she looked away, focused on crushing the potatoes with the metal masher. "You shouldn't end up like me."

Amy's heart caught. It was the first time her mom had ever even come close to talking about her life, acknowledging that things hadn't been as happy as they might have been. It made Amy sad. And a little angry. Those were feelings she'd had to bottle up over the years to keep from upsetting the balance of the house. She'd taken it upon herself to make things cheerful. Felt the weight of the responsibility of it.

Maybe this time they could have a real conversation. But it was hard. She was afraid of saying the wrong thing…again.

"Mom, I know Dad leaving hurt you. But you stopped living, and that makes me sad. It's like…" She took a breath and proceeded as gently as she could. "It's like you gave up."

"I did," Mary murmured, putting the masher in the sink and leaving the potatoes. "I did give up."

Amy asked the question she'd always wanted to. "Are the rumors true, Mom? Was there someone else?"

But Mary shook her head. "Maybe if there'd been another woman I might have understood. The grass is always greener and all that. But nothing tempted him away, Amy. He just didn't love me anymore."

"Or me," Amy said quietly.

Her mother didn't answer. The fact that he'd walked out on them both was clear enough.

"It hurt me, too," she whispered.

"Of course it did. You should have had a father growing up. Instead you were stuck with me...."

Amy's heart was pounding hard. Talking about her emotions was never easy. It was a good way to get hurt. She was smart enough to know it was why she put on the "good-time girl" facade. Don't let anyone see any vulnerability. Don't give them any power. She went to her mom and put her hand on Mary's arm. "I wasn't *stuck* with you. You were a good mother. You were just unhappy. I knew it. I couldn't fix it and you'd never talk about it."

"It hurt too much."

Amy removed her hand. "But weren't you angry? Sometimes I'm angry for you. Sometimes at you, do you understand? Because I wanted you to pull yourself up and start living again. Trying to be happy for both of us was exhausting."

Mary sighed. "Oh, honey, it wasn't your job to take that on, and I'm sorry. The truth is I never wanted to put my feelings on you, but I guess I did that anyway."

"Yes, you did. And anytime I suggested talking it through you shut me down. Can we at least talk now? I'm a big girl. I can handle it."

Mary smiled a little. "You go away a week and come back making decisions and demands."

"I found a little gumption." She couldn't help but smile back. "I realized I was doing the same thing over and over. Looking for approval. Searching for someone to love me instead of worrying about becoming someone I'd like to be."

"Good gracious." Mary looked shocked.

"It's a little Dr. Phil, I realize that," Amy responded with a small laugh. "And it didn't happen overnight. It's been coming for a while. Meeting Jack was just the catalyst, you know? He…he gave me confidence to finally stand up and do something about it."

He really had. And she'd walked away without thanking him for it.

Her smile faded as she returned to the tough questions. "Mom, you were so young when Dad left. Why did you give up? You might have found someone else. Made good friends. Instead you hid yourself away in this house. In your cubicle…"

Supper was getting cold but neither of them cared. It was a conversation that had been needed for far too long. Mary blinked a few times. "When he left, he told me I was a poor excuse for a woman. Silly and boring and he couldn't stand the thought of being cooped up here with me another day."

Amy went to a chair, pulled it out from the table and sat down. "Oh, Mom. What a heartless thing to say."

Mary came over and sat, too. "I loved him. I believed him. I'd made my world around him and I failed. I was depressed, Amy. I know I wasn't fun to be around. We'd tried to have more kids but none came. He was not a small-town kind of guy. It wasn't good enough for him here. I wasn't enough, either."

"But Mom, that was his flaw, not yours."

Mary smiled weakly. "Bless you for saying that."

"You still use your married name."

"We never officially divorced. Made it difficult to

date. Though I expect I might have used that as an excuse. So I wouldn't have to put myself out there again."

Amy blinked. It had never truly occurred to her that her parents were still married.

"Do you want to be?"

"I'm sorry?"

It felt awkward but Amy moved her hand and put it on top of her mom's fingers. "Do you want to be divorced? Start over? It's not too late. There must be in-absentia laws or something. You could see a lawyer. Cami Sanchez could help you out."

"I don't know. After all this time…"

"You're not even fifty. You can't let something he said years ago rule your life." Amy sighed and met her mother's eyes. "I know what they say about me around town. I'm silly and a flirt. I'm sure you've heard, too. It's how I've protected myself from letting anyone too close. But now…"

Her voice trailed off. Now she wasn't so afraid. Jack had hurt her but she'd survived. And she'd stood up for herself. Even though it hadn't ended well, she was glad she hadn't settled for whatever paltry bit of himself Jack was offering.

"It's this Jack person, isn't it?" Mary patted her hand. "Your face changes when you think about him. Your eyes light up when you talk about him."

Amy nodded. "I fell for him. I fell for him despite the fact that I knew there was absolutely no chance for a future together. I didn't see him as a potential husband. Didn't see him as my emotional savior, either. I think he's a bigger wreck than I am." She smiled sadly. "Which is why I said goodbye and came back early."

She squeezed her mom's fingers. "We can both be stronger, can't we? I'm a big girl now. You don't need to protect me. You don't need to be sad. And you definitely don't have to believe what he said."

"Easier said than done."

"Tell me about it." Amy released her mom's fingers. Leaving Jack had been the right thing to do. Didn't stop her from thinking about him all the time, though. Didn't stop her from wishing it might have been different.

"Let's put dinner in the fridge for tomorrow, Mom. I want you to go put on a nice sweater and I'm going to take you out for supper. Not the diner, either. Let's go for Italian. We'll order pasta and have a glass of wine. Just us."

"Oh, honey…"

It seemed like a moment where things were on a knife-edge; to one side was the way things had always been and on the other was the way things might become if they tried. Amy swallowed. She couldn't remember the last time her mom had gone anywhere other than the post office or grocery store. "We deserve a treat," she said softly. "And I'd like to take my mom out to dinner. I'll put this stuff in the fridge while you change."

There was an indecisive moment where Amy was sure Mary was going to refuse.

"All right. I suppose we could do that. I'll just be a moment."

Something blossomed in Amy's chest as she watched her mother leave the room, a pretty blush coloring the older woman's cheeks. As she dug out plastic dishes for the food, she realized what that something was. It was hope.

JACK PAID THE check at the Wagon Wheel diner and stood, shrugging into his coat. The freezing air that had pushed its way into Montana had abated up here, and while still wintry at least he didn't feel like he was going to freeze any exposed skin. He turned up the collar of his coat as he pushed his way out of the diner toward the rental car he'd picked up at the airport. He had a choice now that the papers were signed. He could head back to Aspen Valley or he could make a pit stop.

Maybe he'd just drive by the flower shop and see if she was there. He didn't have to go in. Didn't need to see how she was doing. Just because he'd had the crazy idea to offer her a job didn't mean he had to go through with it.

He tapped his fingers on the steering wheel. Damn girl had surprised the heck out of him, walking away like that. She had a core of strength he hadn't anticipated. What made it worse was that she'd been 100 percent right. About him, about them, about everything.

He parked across the street from the shop and debated going in. He didn't know what to say, didn't know whether to tell her the reason for his visit or not. Word would get out soon enough, he supposed. It was a small town. He didn't exactly want her to hear through the grapevine.

And he couldn't very well avoid her forever. After all, he was going to be spending more time in town between his new investment and his brother and family. Even if the job offer weren't on his mind, they'd be running into each other, wouldn't they?

Resolutely he got out of the car, shut the door and crossed the street. The bell dinged above the door as he entered and the sweet, cloying smell of lilies and roses hit his nostrils.

But instead of Amy behind the counter, it was Melissa Stone. "Jack! Good afternoon. What are you doing back in these parts?"

He regained his composure and smiled warmly. "I was looking for Amy, actually. Is she working today?"

"Afraid not. It's her day off."

"Oh." So much for that, then.

"You can always try her at home. I think she said she had an appointment this morning. She's probably back now."

He nodded. "Thanks." His gaze lit on the flowers in the cooler. "Those flowers there, what are those? The red and pink and orange ones."

"Oh, the gerberas? They're cheerful, aren't they?"

"Can you do some up for me?"

Melissa's smile told him he wasn't fooling anyone. "Of course. I'll put in extra red. Those are Amy's favorites."

There was no sense correcting her when she was right.

He paid for the flowers and headed straight to her house. Two cars were parked in the short driveway so he pulled up along the curb. For some reason his heart was clubbing along at double time. This was silly. It was just Amy.

Only nothing about Amy was *just Amy*. He was fairly certain she had no idea what she'd done. How much she'd turned his life upside down.

He knocked on the door, heard footsteps approach. But it wasn't Amy who answered. It was her mother; a woman who looked much like her daughter only older, and faded. Like she might have once been beautiful, but time and circumstance had taken their toll. She smiled at him, though, which came as a surprise considering what Amy had told him about her mom.

"You must be Amy's Jack," Mary said. "Please come in."

He stepped inside the small foyer, the words *Amy's Jack* causing a strange warmth inside him. The house was small; a plain bungalow with eggshell walls, a few old pictures and carpet that was long past new. It was only a few steps up from shabby, and he reminded himself that Amy's mother had been supporting herself and her daughter on whatever salary she'd had over the years. It wasn't much wonder the woman looked tired. And the house was scrupulously clean. He smiled down at her and held out the triangular brown paper package. "For you, Mrs. Wilson."

Amy would understand. It was worth it to see the older woman's eyes light up as she ran a fingernail under the tape and peeked inside. "Oh, they're lovely. Thank you. And it's just Mary. Not Mrs. Wilson."

"Mom? Who're you talking to?"

Jack's pulse leaped at the sound of Amy's voice from the back of the house. He straightened and shoved his hands into his coat pockets just to give them something to do.

Amy stopped at the end of the hallway and stared up at him. "Jack."

"Hey. Hope it's okay that I stopped by."

That was good, right? Cool. Casual. Unlike the feeling rushing through him at the mere sight of her. Maybe offering her a job wasn't the best idea. But then…surely this feeling would pass.

"I didn't know you were planning to be in town."

Her blue eyes sparkled up at him and he told himself to proceed with caution. No sense in giving her false hope. The flowers had been on impulse but he was glad now he'd given them to her mother—who he realized was watching them curiously.

"I had a meeting this morning, and lunch with Callum and Taylor."

"A meeting in Cadence Creek? What for?"

He forced a smile. "Actually, that's what I wanted to talk to you about."

Mary backed away. "I'll just put these in some water, and then I've got to get going. I have a hair appointment in thirty minutes. Amy, should I put some coffee on for your guest?"

Jack shook his head. "Don't go to any trouble for me, Mrs... Mary."

She nodded and disappeared into the kitchen. Amy came forward, her brow wrinkled in a frown. "What are you doing here, Jack?"

"Your mom is very nice," he said, wanting to ease into the conversation. "She doesn't have to leave, though."

Amy's face relaxed a little. "She really does have an appointment at the salon. There've been some changes since I got back. Good ones."

"Oh?"

"We went to see a lawyer this morning. She's finally taking steps to divorce my dad."

Jack blinked. In normal circumstances those words would be a bad thing, but Jack knew that in this situation it meant steps forward. "You must be pleased about that."

"We talked," she said simply. "I feel better about leaving her in the fall, if she keeps this up."

"About that..." he began.

Mary came back in, went to the closet and took out her coat. "There are some cookies in the tin on the counter, Amy. I'll be back in a couple of hours."

"Okay, Mum."

"Nice to meet you, Jack."

He stood up. "And you. I'm sure I'll see you again soon."

Her eyes lit up. "That's good. 'Bye now."

The house was strangely quiet after she shut the door. He turned back to find Amy watching him, a wary look in her eyes. "See her again soon? What's going on, Jack? Why were you really here in Cadence Creek?"

I came for you. The words seemed loud in his brain even though they never passed his lips. He rejected the idea and pressed forward.

"Let's sit down," he suggested.

He sat on the sofa, hoping she'd sit beside him, but she didn't. She chose a chair across from him, a scarred coffee table between them. It was covered with a lace doily. It seemed like the wrong place for a woman like Amy. She deserved to be in a house with pretty things and lots of color and personality. Like her.

"You're really worried about leaving your mom, aren't you?"

Amy nodded. "As much as I've wanted to get out of the house, I hate the thought of her being here alone. She had such a hard time when Dad left. I feel like I'm abandoning her a little."

Jack smiled. This was perfect. "What if you didn't have to leave her? What if you could be closer to her than you planned?"

She frowned. "What are you talking about, Jack?"

He straightened his shoulders. This would work out just fine. Amy would have her independence, and a good job, and still be able to be close to her mom. He wouldn't have to worry about her at all.

"Remember when I was here at Christmas, and I said I had some meetings in addition to wedding and family stuff?"

"Vaguely."

He nodded. "The ranch out past Cooper Ford's place. The one that went into foreclosure last year? I just closed on it."

Her lips dropped open. And she didn't look happy. He

wasn't sure why he'd expected her to, but he was disappointed just the same.

"You just…up and bought it?"

"I was interested as far back as early December, when I first came for wedding stuff. Sam and Ty were talking about it and how the place had been vacant for several months, the fields lying fallow. It was a real waste but it was tied up in legalities a long time and then it hadn't sold."

"What are you going to do with it, Jack? How many homes do you need? Vancouver, Aspen Valley and now here?"

"I hardly spend any time in Vancouver now. It doesn't count."

But it did. At least he knew it did to her. Never had the differences between them been more marked than right now, with him sitting in her very plain living room. He'd paid well over a million for that ranch and considered it a bargain. Amy's house would have cost less than a tenth of that. They lived in two very different realities. And yet… if you stripped all that away he knew they had something very much in common. Neither of them liked to show the world who they really were. The closest he'd come to letting down his guard was when they were together.

"You know I enjoy Aspen Valley far more than endless boardroom meetings and sales reports. I don't want to sell Shepard Sports—it's too profitable and not good business sense, at least not now. But I'm mixing things up. I'm looking at changing the management structure there. Putting someone else in charge. That way I can focus on what I really enjoy." He met her gaze. "Why did I bother making all this money if I don't take time to use it to be happy?"

"And the ranch makes you happy."

He should have been able to answer with an unqualified yes. And a month ago he probably would have. But something had changed. An unsettledness he couldn't explain, other than it had happened just about the time Callum had gotten married. It had been pretty amazing, seeing his big brother as a husband and dad. And Taylor, too, so in love with Rhys these days. Perhaps he would have been able to put it all in perspective except for one thing: Amy. Getting to know her had changed everything, as much as he didn't want to admit it.

And yet the thought of telling her the whole truth made his insides seize. He'd never told anyone the entire story about his relationship with Sheila. Not in all the years since his accident. It hurt too much.

He pressed forward with the plan he'd rehearsed in the car. "I want to start a similar program at this ranch as I have in Montana. I've already worked up a short list of names for people who could run the team-building part. One is a former football coach I know who does life skills coaching now. But I'd need someone to oversee the hospitality end. There's work to be done to both the house and facilities, of course. Even with a rush on it, summer will be the earliest it'll be ready for bookings. But the business manager's job is yours, Amy, if you want it. You could live on-site, in your own suite. You'd have your independence and still be close enough to check in on your mom. Make sure things are okay."

His speech was greeted with silence. She was staring at him as if he were a stranger, and for the first time ever he couldn't tell what she was thinking.

"You came here to offer me a job?"

He shifted on the sofa cushion. "Well, yes. I don't have any doubts you could do it. The operation here would likely be bigger—there's a large cabin on the property, as well, and there'd be more staff to oversee. We could hire housekeeping and cooking staff, and leave you to the administration and hostess end of things. You were so great with making our guests comfortable and welcome, and you whipped the office into shape in no time. You're a natural."

He smiled at her.

"That's what you came to offer me. Employment."

He frowned. "Didn't you just ask that?"

"I was looking for confirmation. Because I thought maybe I hadn't heard you right."

"You did." It was hard to keep the smile on his face when he felt as if he were somehow walking into a minefield.

She folded her hands in her lap. "We made love, Jack. We shouldn't pretend that it was just sex. It wasn't. And the kiss you gave me at the airport wasn't exactly platonic. So for you to come here and offer me a job…I'm not sure if I'm surprised, disappointed or insulted."

"Insulted?" He got up from the sofa and put his hands on his hips. "I'm offering the perfect solution. The fact that I'd entrust this to you is insulting?"

She looked up at him. "What's it supposed to be, Jack, my consolation prize?"

He felt as if she'd struck him. Not because he was offended but because he suspected on some level she was right. It was his way of trying to make things up to her. Of doing something for her so he didn't have to…

The room felt like it was closing in on him. His lungs squeezed as he tried to get enough air but couldn't. Amy had a way of hitting just a little too close with her honesty. He was offering this so he didn't have to give up any part of himself.

"I wouldn't offer it to you if I didn't think you were

right for the job," he managed to say. He met her gaze and forced himself to hold it even though the need to escape was pulsing through him.

"And if I were a different person, if I were the woman I was even two months ago, I'd say yes, with a big elaborate plan about how it would keep me close to you so I could convince you that I was the right woman for you."

"But you're not."

"I'm not that woman," she confirmed. "Not anymore. Will you sit back down again? You're making me nervous."

He sat, resting his hands on his knees. He was still offended at her remark about being insulted. That hadn't been his intention at all. While he was scared to death of an actual relationship, it stung a bit that she was so determined to *not* be with him. Turning it down didn't seem to be bothering her all that much. She had no idea how torn up he was inside. The word *love* had popped into his head so many times he was getting tired of shoving it down again.

"I'm sorry, Jack. I've got to refuse your offer, though I'm sure it's a great opportunity. But I'm going to go to school to get my diploma and find a job all on my own. Mom and I will manage. I'll only be forty-five minutes away."

"You're turning it down? Because you feel, what, like you're getting special treatment?"

To his surprise her eyes filled with tears. "No, you stupid ass. I'm turning it down because it would be horribly unfair to me to be tied to you day in and day out and not be yours when I'm so completely in love with you."

It was a good thing he was sitting down because it felt like the floor disappeared from beneath his feet.

He said the only words that came to him. "You can't be in love with me. You can't."

Chapter Thirteen

Amy knew it would be like this but beating around the bush just wasn't working. Seeing him today had been like a punch to the gut. She'd come back to Cadence Creek and made decisions and felt good about her plans but something was missing. That something was Jack. Being with him had changed her. It had been too wonderful, felt too much like the real thing. No matter what had come before making love or after, for that blissful night it had been as real as it could get. Souls had been bared without words needing to be said. The only answer was that she must have fallen in love with him…against her best intentions. It had never been like that for her before. Not ever. A part of her wondered if it ever would be again.

And that part of her was what had told her she could never settle for pieces of Jack. She needed everything or nothing.

"I can, and do," she said, swallowing the tears clogged in her throat. "But I know you don't love me back. Working for you would be torture, day in and day out. Knowing—" she choked a little "—and not having. It wouldn't be fair to either of us."

"What do you want, then? I told you from the beginning I don't do relationships and love and marriage and all that."

"Yes, you did. It's not your fault. You didn't change the rules, Jack. I did. I was so bent on being different, on having something to prove, that I went too far in the other direction. The truth is the outgoing, bubbly Amy that was here before and the determined, goal-focused Amy that was at Aspen Valley aren't really me. The real Amy Wilson is somewhere in between. I may want to break free of old habits and exert my independence, but that doesn't change who I am inside. And that person wants a husband, and a family, and a home someday. The kind of life I never had growing up. If you aren't the kind of man who I can see in that role, I'm wasting my time— not to mention my heart."

His face paled. She hadn't meant to hurt him. She just wanted to be honest.

"I don't want to be needy, and clingy and…small. Does that make sense? I want to discover things. See places, meet people. But it would be nice to do that with a partner by my side. I won't be like my mom, Jack. I won't live my life beating myself up about it, wondering what I might have done differently so you'd love me. I know you had your heart broken. I don't know why you can't move past it, but you can't."

"She had an abortion."

The room dropped into silence.

Amy stared at him. The color was back in his cheeks. Too much color, she realized. He hadn't meant to say it. It had just come out. But it was out there now and she wasn't going to ignore it.

"Who did? Sheila?"

He rose. "Forget I said anything. I should go."

She jumped up and grabbed his arm. "Oh, no, you don't. You can't drop a bomb like that and run away."

She lifted her chin and met his eyes. "Talk to me,"

she said quietly. "You know I don't judge. Just talk to me, Jack. Sheila was pregnant, wasn't she? That's why it hurt so much?"

He looked down into her eyes for a long moment. She could see the longing there, the need for him to unburden himself of the secret and also the urge to hide away again. She squeezed his arm with her fingers, trying to reassure him.

He nodded, almost imperceptibly, but she saw the affirmation. "She told me a month before we left for France."

Once he said it, his muscles relaxed beneath her hand.

He sat heavily on the sofa, and this time she sat beside him, her hand resting reassuringly on his thigh. Maybe he'd hurt her but he'd given her a great gift, too. Opportunity. New horizons. She owed him even if it simply meant being a friend.

"Was that when you decided to finish out the season and leave your coach?"

He nodded. "You have to understand what he was like. So driven, but really likable in public. Charming. Well-respected. No one had any idea what he was like in private. I idolized him—until I saw the bruises on her arms one day before she could cover up."

"He hurt her?"

"Yes."

"And you fell in love with her. Didn't you worry about what would happen if he found out?"

Jack looked straight ahead, his jaw a hard line. "Yes. All the time."

He was quiet for so long she had to nudge him. "What happened in France, Jack?"

He turned his head, a quick motion that told her she'd

interrupted some thought or memory. "France?" His lips pursed. "I really don't want to talk about this."

"You need to. You need to tell someone what happened. Does Callum know?"

He shook his head.

"No one?"

"Not a soul."

"But Jack. Something this big is too much to carry around on your own." She lifted her hand and touched his cheek. "You can trust me. You know that, don't you?"

His eyes closed for a minute. His throat bobbed as if he were having trouble swallowing. "I knew she was pregnant. We had to keep it quiet, but I'd worked it all out. I was telling her how it was all going to go down after the season was done. I'd fire him and she would leave him and we'd be together. We'd raise the baby together. We just had to make it through the rest of the season without him suspecting. But she said she couldn't. That he'd kill her if he found out she was carrying another man's child." His voice went flat, as if removing the emotion would somehow make the next words easier to say. "And she told me that she'd already taken care of it."

"She'd terminated the pregnancy." Amy's stomach seemed to drop to her feet. Abortion was so…final.

"Without even telling me, without talking to me about it. Without giving me a chance to change her mind…. It was like I didn't even enter the equation."

"Oh, Jack. You wanted the baby?"

"I wanted them both," he confessed, his voice raw.

She knew he wasn't aware that a tear had escaped the corner of his eye and was running down his cheek. "And then you blew out your knee, ending your career…."

Jack shook his head. "No. First we got caught by a photographer and a picture showed up in a tabloid. And then Chase confronted her and I interrupted their argument. It escalated from there. I told him if he ever touched her again that I'd kill him. And then I told her we were leaving."

"And did she leave with you?"

"No." The word was flat. "I might have forgiven the abortion in time. I was hurt and angry but I did understand that her reality was twisted and she was afraid. I offered her a way out, Amy. I would have quit skiing right then. Would've forgotten about qualifying for another Olympics or being on the podium for the World Cup. I would have gotten on a plane and taken us both home. But she didn't say anything. She just stood there, looking at the floor." His voice caught. "I offered her a way out and she didn't take it. She chose him. I still don't understand how she could do that."

So many things became clear for Amy then. His rescue complex, for one. While she was at the ranch she'd heard about how he'd stepped in and saved it and most of the jobs of the employees, as well. She knew he'd taken care of all of Rosa's expenses after her accident. He'd come into the country club bathroom and saved her embarrassment and given her a job. All the time trying to make up for the one person he hadn't been able to save.

"I'm so sorry, Jack."

He shrugged. "I was so stunned that I let down my guard. And that was when he hit me."

He lifted his hand and touched the scar by his ear. "I should have seen it coming. His ring cut me. I didn't fight back and he hit me again. The blow gave me a concussion. I should never have competed. I knew I didn't feel right, but at that point skiing was all I had left. It was the only thing that made sense. I blacked out on the training run and went down. And *that's* when I blew the knee."

"And so you lost everything."

"Yes. And now you know why I don't talk about it. It was not my finest hour."

He put his elbows on his knees. She'd never seen him this way—utterly resigned. He was always larger than life. Take-charge. Even when he was more relaxed at the ranch, there was a confidence about him that was missing right now.

She tried to offer a different perspective. "I can't speak for Sheila, but sometimes it's easier to stay where you are, even if it's not a good place, if what is waiting for you is scary. The unknown can be pretty intimidating."

"You did it."

She smiled a little. "But not until I was ready. And you gave me the shove I needed. Besides, I had nothing as traumatic as spousal abuse to deal with either, Jack."

"I know." He sighed. "But I can't help but think that my son or daughter would have been in school by now. Might have had my hair or her eyes. And I'll never know, you know?"

She rubbed his back and blinked back tears. She'd known he had his heart broken but hadn't figured it was something like this. She hadn't even realized he liked kids, or wanted his own. It was a new dimension to Jack that only added to her depth of feeling for him. He was so extraordinary, but unless he was willing to meet her halfway, she knew deep down that it would never work. And that hurt her more than anything.

"Do you still love her, Jack?" She held her breath, waiting for his answer.

"No. Sometimes I wonder if I ever really loved her at all or if I just got caught up in the situation. But I must have. Otherwise it wouldn't have hurt so much. Otherwise I wouldn't be so afraid to..."

He broke off, as if he'd finally realized he'd said too much. But Amy picked up on it and pressed forward. "Afraid to what?"

He looked over at her. His eyes were unreadable, distant, as if he'd put a wall up between the words he was saying and the emotion behind them. "Afraid to give myself to anyone again. It wasn't just the leaving. I was betrayed and the cost was almost too much for me to take. I never want to put myself in that position again. I'll never give anyone the power to hurt me like that again."

Amy's heart sank. For all his confiding in her, there really was no hope, was there? It would be so easy to give in. To fool herself into believing she could reach him in time. It's what she normally would do.

But this time was different. Not just because she'd become stronger. But because in all the years she'd been searching, she'd never felt like this before. Not even with Terry. She loved Jack not with the idealistic eyes of a girl, but with the heart of a woman. With all his attributes and flaws.

"If I thought being with you on whatever terms you set would take away your pain, I'd gladly do it. But that's up to you. You have to want to move on. You don't want to because if you don't move on, then you don't forget either the pain or the love. Because somehow you see forgetting as a betrayal."

"Amy…"

"And so you spend your time building things and moving from one thing to another trying to find contentment and you never quite find it. You rescue people to make up for the one time you couldn't. I love you, Jack, but I can't be another one of your causes. You'd eventually move on and I'd just be…left behind."

He sighed. "I wish I could tell you you're wrong. I do care for you, Amy. The time we spent together…it's the closest I've been to someone since her." Pain was etched on his face as he let her down in the kindest way possible. "You're beautiful and kind and way smarter than you give yourself credit for. But you were right back in Montana when you said you needed someone who was going to meet you in the middle. I'm not sure I'll ever be ready to do that."

It felt very final. A heavy weight settled in the pit of her stomach; there was no reason to keep him from walking out the door now. At least they'd talked. At least she understood. She didn't even blame him. Everyone had their baggage to drag around, their personal crosses to bear.

He got up from the sofa. "I really should go."

"I'll walk you out."

At the front door he paused. "The job is still yours if you want it. You don't need to decide now. I thought it would be a way for you to do something you're good at and still be close to home for your mom."

The consideration made her heart ache. "Thanks, Jack. I'll let you know if I change my mind."

Their gazes clung for a long moment, a sequence of breaths in which she replayed that beautiful night in her mind once more. He could be giving and open if he would just let himself go and learn to trust again. But if she'd learned anything from her parents' failed marriage, it was that it didn't work when one person gave more, loved more, wished more.

And so she let him go. And shut the door.

Chapter Fourteen

Something felt off. Jack should have hit the highway and made for the airport, but instead he found himself heading just out of town toward Callum's.

Hell of a time to need his big brother.

He pulled into the driveway of Callum's farm and took a moment to look around. The house was small, but in the spring they were planning on adding a piece and expanding their family. There was nothing out of place around the barn, which sported a fresh coat of paint. His brother was happy, doing what he wanted, with a fine, pretty wife and an adorable daughter.

But a year ago he'd been hiding away, licking his wounds over a broken engagement and nursing his guilt over some accident on his last deployment. How had he moved past all that to happiness?

Jack shivered in the cold as he walked up to the front door and knocked. Avery answered, looking radiant and happy with an angelic Nell in her arms.

"Jack! We weren't expecting you. Come on in. Callum's just having some coffee before going out to milk."

"Thanks." He stepped inside. The house was warm and smelled like chocolate cake. Avery had probably been baking. "Sorry to just drop in…"

"Don't be silly. You're welcome anytime. Heard you closed on the ranch deal."

He smiled. "Yeah."

Callum came in from the kitchen. "Hey, bro. What brings you by? You forget something at lunch?"

"You got a few minutes?"

"I was just heading to the barn, but you're welcome to join me. If you're not afraid of getting your pretty clothes dirty."

"Shut up. And lend me a pair of boots."

Callum's fast grin made Jack feel better. He and his brother hadn't been all that close for a while, but lately they'd gotten closer. He took off his shoes and shoved his feet into the boots Callum took from a small closet, then traded his jacket for a heavy denim one that Callum handed over.

"I'll be back in for dinner." Callum gave Nell and Avery a quick kiss.

"You staying, Jack? There's plenty."

"Naw. I'll need to be heading back to the airport. Thanks, though."

He ruffled Nell's hair and gave Avery a smile.

He thought of Sheila...briefly. And then thought of Amy. Her blond, shiny curls, and how she'd look holding a golden, curly-headed baby in her arms.

His insides tumbled around uneasily.

The inside of the barn was warmer than Jack expected, sheltered from the icy wind. Callum turned on a radio, the soft sounds of a local country station filling the milking parlor. Jack had spent enough time at their uncle's, too, to know how things worked. For a few minutes they worked in silence, bringing in the first cows and hooking them up to the milking machines.

"You got something on your mind, Jack?" Callum looked over and raised an eyebrow.

"You could say that." Talking about his feelings was never easy, but he thought maybe Callum would understand, considering how badly Jane had hurt him when she'd broken off their engagement only weeks after he'd returned from overseas. "You're happy, right?"

Callum chuckled. "I've been married what, six weeks? I think that still qualifies as the honeymoon period."

Jack grinned. "Yeah. But…before that. How did you… I mean, you went through a lot. How did you get to a place where you could trust Avery?"

Callum's gaze sharpened. "This about you and Amy? Or you and Sheila?"

Jack shoved his hands into his jacket pockets. "Both, I guess. Amy and I, we…" He frowned. "I don't know what we are."

"You love her?"

Jack shrugged.

Callum's expression grew concerned. "I spent a lot of time thinking about all the reasons why I couldn't trust Avery because of what Jane did. But she wasn't Jane. Amy's not Sheila, either."

"So how did you get past it?" Jack looked up, wondering if Callum had a magic bullet for moving beyond the past. He hoped to God he did, because all this confusion was getting annoying. He talked himself in and out of his feelings all day long and never came to any good conclusion.

Callum was quiet for a while. They unhooked the first cows, released them from the parlor and brought in the next, cleaning the udders and hooking them up.

The rhythmic sound of the milking machine and the radio filled the comfortable room. "It wasn't easy. And

I nearly screwed it up for good. She left and went back to Ontario and took Nell with her."

Jack gaped. He hadn't known that. "What happened?"

Callum smiled. "I realized that there was something worse than risking getting hurt again."

"What was that?"

Callum put a hand on Jack's shoulder. "Living the rest of my life without her."

Jack couldn't move. The words rippled through him, sounding so right it was terrifying. Nothing had been the same since he'd followed Amy into that restroom at the wedding. He'd told himself all sorts of things, but the moment she'd tossed her hair back and followed him onto the dance floor something had changed.

"Scary as hell, isn't it?"

Callum's voice interrupted Jack's thoughts. Dazed, Jack stared at his brother. "What did you do?"

"I packed a bag and planned to go after her. Only she showed up on my doorstep first. Turned out she couldn't live without me, either. Made it a whole lot less scary."

Jack shook his head, his thoughts settling. "Amy's not like that. She showed me the door."

A rich chuckle filled the air. "Avery knows her a lot better than I do, but from what I gather she's a firecracker. And smart, too, if she can see through your legendary charm. No woman in their right mind is going to compete with the woman you can't forget. What'd you do, tell her you'd never let anyone hurt you that way again?"

Heat climbed his neck.

"Oh, for God's sake," Callum chided. "You're an idiot."

"I know that."

Another set of cows was done and they paused to work again, the routine of it comforting. There was a reason

Callum liked farming, a reason Jack enjoyed the ranch. It was simple and constant. In a crazy, mixed-up world, it made sense.

Finally Callum spoke again. "What you've got to ask yourself is, is she going to become the woman you can't forget? Is being without her worse than facing your fear? Because life doesn't have guarantees. Sometimes you have to take a risk to be happy. And if she makes you happy, the hell with the rest."

Jack stared at his brother for a long moment. "I offered her a job," he admitted.

Callum barked out a laugh. "And she turned it down. I like her already."

"She's so determined. She was stuck in a rut here for a long time, but when she made up her mind…boy, there was no changing it."

He realized something about Amy then. Every move she made was deliberately chosen. Even if she moved quickly, as she did with offering to go to Montana, she did it on purpose. Her offer to help. Her insistence that they keep things platonic. And then reversing that decision to be with him. They hadn't fallen into each other's arms by accident. She had *chosen* to. Knowing all along there was no future for them. She'd taken a risk. She'd shared herself with him and he'd handed it back to her as if it had meant nothing when in truth it was everything.

"I've been very, very stupid," he said in a low voice.

"You wouldn't be the first," Callum said. "But I'm pretty sure you can make things right. I saw the way she looked at you at Christmastime."

"I messed it up big-time…."

"Well, then, you've got nothing to lose." Callum nodded. "As it stands now, you've already lost her. It won't get worse. But it could sure get better. If you've got the balls."

Jack punched Callum on the shoulder, and Callum's breath came out in an "oof."

"You got this?"

"Get out of here. Your romantic woes are annoying my cows. Happy cows give more milk." Callum's grin was sideways as he teased his brother.

"Thanks, Callum."

"Let me know how it turns out. There's a bottle of Scotch hidden in the feed room for emergencies."

Jack gave one parting grin before heading out of the milking parlor. He was halfway back to town before he realized he was still wearing Callum's boots and jacket.

AMY PARED THE last potato and put it in the pot for supper. She rinsed the vegetables, put fresh water on them and set them on the burner. All the while she saw Jack's face in her mind, the anguished expression and tortured look in his eyes as he told her about that day so long ago that had shaped everything he'd done since then.

He was so afraid.

She was *this* close to going after him. To throwing caution to the wind and taking a chance. Maybe that was what he needed—someone to believe in him. To stick by him. To trust him the way that Sheila never had.

Then again, was she any better? She was sitting here at home for the same reason—because she was waiting for someone to care enough to fight for her. To be in it for the long haul. Boy, they were quite a pair, weren't they?

Mary reached into the cupboard and took out plates and glasses. "You okay?"

"Fine," she answered quietly. It was the third time Mary had asked since arriving home to find Jack gone.

There was a knock on the door.

"I'll get it," Amy said. At the first knock her heart had jumped and she'd beaten down the automatic hope that sprung up. Jack was gone. She would have to move on.

She opened the door and there he was, in a fleece-lined old denim jacket with a frayed collar and rubber boots. The scent of cows wafted in ahead of him.

"Jack?"

"Can we talk?"

"I was just getting supper."

"Please, Amy. I said stuff this afternoon… There were things I should have said…." He ran his hand over his hair, leaving the curling strands a little on end. "Please."

"Do you want to come in?"

"I thought we could go for a drive. I won't keep you long."

He looked so hopeful she couldn't say no. And that was the problem. It was so hard to say no to Jack, and being around him only made her heart hurt more.

"Let me tell my mom and get a coat."

Mary simply smiled and said she'd save Amy a plate. Amy went to the closet and got boots and a coat and within a couple of minutes found herself in Jack's car as they made their way north.

"Where are we going?"

Jack kept his eyes on the road. "To the new place. I want to show you something."

Her stomach flip-flopped nervously. Was he going to try to change her mind about the job? It was a good offer, she knew that. And it had been considerate, knowing she wanted to stay close to her mom. If it weren't for her pesky feelings for him it would be perfect.

But she couldn't get past the idea of Jack being her boss. Being close enough to touch but off-limits.

"Where did you go after you left my place?"

He smiled a little. "Can't you tell? I was at Callum's. I was halfway back to your house before I realized I still had his stuff on. I was helping him with the milking."

"I thought I smelled eau de Cow."

"Sorry."

She laughed a little. "It's a ranching community. You get used to animal smells."

They left town limits and turned onto a service road, past Cooper Ford's sprawling horse ranch until she saw a lane with a Realtor sign still at the end by the road. Jack's headlights swooped across it as he turned in the driveway. The lane climbed a little until the house came into view at the top of a knoll. Rolling hills were dark shadows in the early evening light, the days so short now in the depths of winter.

The house itself was a large, sprawling log-cabin style with big windows facing northeast. Beyond it was a huge but vacant barn and several outbuildings. All of them empty and lonely-looking.

"What did you want to show me, Jack?"

She turned to him, his face lit by nothing more than the dashboard lights. It reminded her of Christmas Eve, when he'd driven her home from church and she'd asked to go along to Montana with him. Everything had changed.

He didn't say anything. Just looked at her for a long, long moment. Then he reached down, took her hand and placed it along the side of his face. Turned his head into her palm, just a bit, and closed his eyes.

Her heart wept.

"Jack," she whispered. "Please…you're tearing me apart."

With his eyes still closed, he kissed the soft skin at the underside of her thumb. Then he opened his eyes.

"When we were in the bathroom at Callum's wedding, I told you Rhys wasn't worth your tears, remember?"

She nodded. "Yes."

"And I said that you deserved to be with someone who wanted to be with you, and only you. Who couldn't live another day without you. Do you remember that?"

Her throat was tight. "You know I do."

"You are no one's consolation prize, Amy Wilson. Least of all mine. I love you. I love you so much it scares the living daylights out of me and I don't know what to do with myself. I can't stand the thought of being hurt again but I can't bear the idea of being without you for the rest of my life."

"You...love me?"

She hated how the words came out soft and unsure, after all the hard work she'd put in to be strong and self-assured. And yet she needed to hear him say it again. Longed for it. To be sure he meant it.

"I do," he confirmed. "I love you. I didn't realize it at first. All I knew was that I felt better when I was around you. I looked forward to seeing you and God knows I was attracted to you. I did such a good job rationalizing it at first. And then..."

"And then the clock struck midnight," she murmured. "And everything changed."

His eyes glowed at her. "Yes," he said, "everything changed at New Year's. I couldn't hide from you anymore. When we made love...it was more than sex. It was like something fell into place. And it scared me so badly that I acted like a complete ass."

"You're afraid of getting hurt again. I know that, Jack.

And I took such a hard line because I'm so afraid of losing myself again. I want to be strong…."

"You are strong."

"I was such a fool for so long, chasing after rainbows that didn't exist because I was afraid I'd be alone like my mom. But there are worse things than being alone. There's being in love and not having it returned. There's knowing that you will never be enough. I am so determined to not be like my mom. Not because she's weak. But because she's unhappy."

"The question is, are you willing to let yourself be happy? To give me a chance to make you happy?" He squeezed her fingers, lowering her hand from his face and resting it on the seat between them.

"You really mean that." Hope swirled through her.

"I really mean it," he replied. "Callum said something to me today that made so much sense. I asked him how he moved past his fears to be with Avery. And he said it was because being without her was far more frightening than whatever it was holding them apart. I'm asking you to give me a chance. To take a risk on me, and in return I'll do whatever I can to make you happy. If you want to go to school, we'll make that happen. Whatever it takes. Because nothing works without you, Amy. Nothing at all."

She unbuckled her seat belt and slid closer, wishing the car had a bench seat instead of buckets with a console in the middle. "Maybe you could kiss me while I think about it," she answered cheekily, though she knew there wasn't much thinking to be done. The words she'd never thought he'd utter had been said. He loved her. He wanted to be with her. She knew there might be tough roads ahead. But it would be better to travel them together than be apart.

He leaned forward and kissed her. Not the tentative kiss she expected but a wholly encompassing outpouring of emotion that washed away her teasing smile and shook her to her core. This was the man who'd held her in his arms in the dark as they welcomed in a new year. Who had gazed deeply into her eyes as they were joined together, whose heart called out to hers when his voice couldn't.

"I love you," he said when their lips finally parted. "Say I'm not too late."

"You're not too late," she breathed, touching her forehead to his. "You're not too late."

They clung to each other in the confines of the car for a few more minutes until Jack finally let out a breath and straightened. "Come with me. Just for a minute."

"Okay."

They got out of the car and he reached for her hand, guiding her up the rest of the driveway to the house, past the porch and to the backyard. Even in the dark, the starlight illuminated the vastness of the rolling prairie below them. "Ours," he said softly. "If you want it to be. I was thinking we could divide our time between Aspen Valley and here. You'd be close to your mom most of the time and she could always come stay with us from time to time if she wanted. I know that's important to you."

"What about your family?"

He put his arm around her and pulled her into his side. "Callum and Avery and Nell are here. Taylor's moving here to be with Rhys. Other than my parents, my family *is* here."

He looked down at her and she looked up at him, the feeling so utterly right she could hardly believe it was possible.

"Amy," he said gently, "even if they weren't in Cadence Creek, you're here. And that's where my home is. Nothing was the same after you left. You're the piece that's missing."

"Oh, Jack…"

"Those things you wanted…marriage, a home, a family… I think I want them, too. It might take me a little time, but I want to get there. With you, Amy. Only with you. If you'll walk down that road with me."

"Kind of lonely walking it alone," she answered, wrapping her arms around his middle.

He kissed her again, wrapping her in his arms until she could no longer feel the cold winter air on her cheeks or fingertips or toes. He pulled her against his hard length, freer now that the barriers between them were gone and until desire swept through them both, leaving them longing and wanting. His hand crept inside her jacket and beneath her sweater, cool fingers on warm skin. He was hers, she realized. And she was his. Finally.

Jack's lips swept down the column of her neck. "You know, I don't think this is going to be as difficult as I thought."

She couldn't help the smile that blossomed on her lips, a smile of joy and happiness. "That's very good news, but I do have one piece of advice."

He straightened, still holding her close as if afraid to let her go. "Just one?"

She nodded. "You're going to have to get something without bucket seats if I'm not going to be able to keep my hands off you. Like every self-respecting cowboy, you're going to have to invest in a pickup truck."

"Done," he decreed, tightening his hand on her waist. "But I doubt we'll get far. I don't plan on letting you out of my arms for a while yet."

She snuggled into his chest as everything clicked into its proper place.

"Sounds good to me," she answered.

Epilogue

The air around the lodge was filled with the scent of grilling burgers and the sound of laughter. Amy pushed open the French doors to the deck with her hip as she carried two enormous bowls of potato chips for the friends and neighbors gathered at Shepard Lodge for a grand opening barbecue.

She paused for a moment, gazing down at the scene before her. The Diamonds—Sam and Angela, Ty and Clara, Molly, the children. Rhys and Taylor, who'd just returned from their honeymoon, and Callum, watching a toddling Nell with eagle eyes while Avery rested her hand on a noticeably rounded belly. Amy's mother, sitting with Harry and Susan Shepard in the shade of a poplar tree, chatting away and smiling. Melissa and Cooper Ford, also newlyweds, holding hands as they ambled up the dirt path that linked the horse barn to the yard around the house. It was Cooper's fine riding stock grazing in the field in the distance.

Their friends.

And Jack, standing next to a stainless-steel barbecue, spatula in hand as the meat sizzled.

"Nearly ready?" she asked as she put down the bowls.

"Another few minutes," he replied, putting down the lid and hanging the spatula on a hook.

He went to her and slid his arms around her waist. "Glad we decided to hold a party?"

"Absolutely," she replied, lifting her head so she could place a kiss on his lips. There was a confidence and contentment that came from sharing Jack's life—and his heart. It didn't matter what anyone thought or said anymore. She loved him, and he loved her, and that was all that mattered.

She looked down at her hand, the diamond ring sparkling there in the July sunlight. "You know what?" she said, sliding her hands over his ribs and linking them behind his back. She looked up into his eyes. "Let's just have a small wedding. Everyone we love is right here in this yard. Let's do it just like this…before the end of the summer, here at the lodge. We'll get a justice of the peace, Avery can make cupcakes…"

"You know Taylor is going to want to dip her fingers into the planning. She won't be able to help herself."

"She's awesome and efficient. Why not? I mean it, Jack. I don't need a big church wedding. Just us and the people we care about most, and our home."

"What about the honeymoon?"

She smiled. "We could always go to Aspen Valley. Where it all started."

After Jack had proposed, they'd made a decision. Summers they'd spend in Cadence Creek and at Shepard Lodge. Winters, with the proximity to the winter activities, they'd spend in Montana. And down the road, when they had to think about school years for their children, they'd reevaluate.

"Miguel and Rosa would love that."

"As long as we're together, it's all good."

Jack put his palm along her cheek. "You're really okay

with not going to school this fall? You're sure this is what you want?"

"I'm sure." She grinned. "Hey, I waited long enough for you. I'm not going to be separated from you any more than I have to be. Besides, I fully intend to do my learning on the job."

Someone cleared their throat and Amy and Jack turned to see Taylor standing behind them. "Um…I was hoping to get some drinks from the cooler."

Amy and Jack broke apart and Taylor scooted by, opened the cooler and grabbed two sodas.

"Taylor? How long would it take to put together a casual wedding? Say, outdoors, with maybe twenty or thirty guests?"

She frowned. "It would depend on the location and their definition of casual."

Jack pulled Amy close to his side. "Say here? Mid-August?"

Taylor's eyes widened. "Holy cow. I owe Callum twenty bucks. He said you'd have a short engagement, but I bet him it'd be after Christmas. Damn."

Amy laughed. "I'm not about to let your brother get away."

"Let me grab a notebook and we can start making lists."

Amy reached out and touched Taylor's wrist. "Not today. Let's just enjoy the afternoon. I just want to hang out with your family and our friends."

Taylor's face softened. "Honey, *you* are our family."

Jack pressed a kiss to her temple as her eyes started to sting.

"It kills me to say it, but for once my little sister is right."

Taylor squeezed her hand and hopped down the steps.

She hadn't even reached the bottom when they heard her call out, "Hey, Callum, guess what?"

Jack chuckled down low as together they looked out over the land and the people they cared about most.

"Happy?" Jack asked simply.

"Happy," she answered.

* * * * *

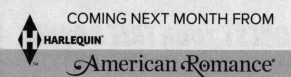
Available March 4, 2014

#1489 THE TEXAS WILDCATTER'S BABY
McCabe Homecoming
by Cathy Gillen Thacker

Environmentalist Rand McCabe embarks on a passionate affair with lady wildcatter Ginger Rollins, but can't convince her to begin a real relationship with him...until she finds herself unexpectedly pregnant with his child.

#1490 MOST ELIGIBLE SHERIFF
Sweetheart, Nevada
by Cathy McDavid

Ruby McPhee switches places with her twin sister so she can lay low in Sweetheart, Nevada. She doesn't expect complications—except it turns out Ruby is "dating" Cliff Dempsey, local sheriff and the town's most eligible bachelor!

#1491 AIMING FOR THE COWBOY
Fatherhood
by Mary Leo

An unexpected pregnancy hog-ties Helen Shaw's rodeo career and friendship with future father Colt Granger. The sexy cowboy's proposal sounds sweet, but is it the real deal?

#1492 ROPING THE RANCHER
by Julie Benson

Colt Montgomery has sworn off women after his ex left him to raise his teenage daughter alone. When actress Stacy Michaels shows up at his ranch, she tests his resolve to steer clear of women!

YOU CAN FIND MORE INFORMATION ON UPCOMING HARLEQUIN® TITLES, FREE EXCERPTS AND MORE AT WWW.HARLEQUIN.COM.

HARCNM0214

REQUEST YOUR FREE BOOKS!
2 FREE NOVELS PLUS 2 FREE GIFTS!

HARLEQUIN®

American ★ Romance®

LOVE, HOME & HAPPINESS

YES! Please send me 2 FREE Harlequin® American Romance® novels and my 2 FREE gifts (gifts are worth about $10). After receiving them, if I don't wish to receive any more books, I can return the shipping statement marked "cancel." If I don't cancel, I will receive 4 brand-new novels every month and be billed just $4.74 per book in the U.S. or $5.24 per book in Canada. That's a savings of at least 14% off the cover price! It's quite a bargain! Shipping and handling is just 50¢ per book in the U.S. and 75¢ per book in Canada.* I understand that accepting the 2 free books and gifts places me under no obligation to buy anything. I can always return a shipment and cancel at any time. Even if I never buy another book, the two free books and gifts are mine to keep forever.

154/354 HDN F4YN

Name _____ (PLEASE PRINT) _____

Address _____ Apt. # _____

City _____ State/Prov. _____ Zip/Postal Code _____

Signature (if under 18, a parent or guardian must sign)

Mail to the **Harlequin® Reader Service:**
IN U.S.A.: P.O. Box 1867, Buffalo, NY 14240-1867
IN CANADA: P.O. Box 609, Fort Erie, Ontario L2A 5X3

Want to try two free books from another line?
Call 1-800-873-8635 or visit www.ReaderService.com.

* Terms and prices subject to change without notice. Prices do not include applicable taxes. Sales tax applicable in N.Y. Canadian residents will be charged applicable taxes. Offer not valid in Quebec. This offer is limited to one order per household. Not valid for current subscribers to Harlequin American Romance books. All orders subject to credit approval. Credit or debit balances in a customer's account(s) may be offset by any other outstanding balance owed by or to the customer. Please allow 4 to 6 weeks for delivery. Offer available while quantities last.

Your Privacy—The Harlequin® Reader Service is committed to protecting your privacy. Our Privacy Policy is available online at www.ReaderService.com or upon request from the Harlequin Reader Service.

We make a portion of our mailing list available to reputable third parties that offer products we believe may interest you. If you prefer that we not exchange your name with third parties, or if you wish to clarify or modify your communication preferences, please visit us at www.ReaderService.com/consumerchoice or write to us at Harlequin Reader Service Preference Service, P.O. Box 9062, Buffalo, NY 14269. Include your complete name and address.

HAR13R

*Ruby McPhee is hiding out in Sweetheart, Nevada, having
changed places with her twin sister. What her sister didn't
tell her is that Scarlett was dating the town sheriff!
But what happens after Cliff Dempsey figures this out?
Find out in* MOST ELIGIBLE SHERIFF
by Cathy McDavid.

Picking up the bouquet, Cliff said, "These are for you."

"Thanks." Scarlett accepted the flowers and, with both
hands full, set them back down on the table. "You didn't have
to."

"They're a bribe. I was hoping you'd go with me to the
square dance Friday night."

The community center had finally reopened nearly a year
after the fire. The barbecue and dance were in celebration.

"I...um...don't think I can. I appreciate the invitation,
though."

"Are you going with someone else?" He didn't like the
idea of that.

"No, no. I'm just...busy." She clutched her mug tightly
between both hands.

"I'd really like to take you." Fifteen minutes ago he probably
wouldn't have put up a fight and would have accepted her loss
of interest. Except he was suddenly more interested in her
than before. "Think on it overnight."

"O-kay." She took another sip of her coffee. As she did, the
cuff of her shirtsleeve pulled back.

He saw it then, a small tattoo on the inside of her left wrist resembling a shooting star. A jolt coursed through him. He hadn't seen the tattoo before.

Because seven days ago, when he and Scarlett ate dinner at the I Do Café, it hadn't been there.

"Is that new?" He pointed to the tattoo.

Panic filled her eyes. "Um…yeah. It is."

Cliff didn't buy her story. There were no tattoo parlors in Sweetheart and, to his knowledge, she hadn't left town. And why the sudden panic?

Scarlett averted her face. She was hiding something.

Leaning down, he smelled her hair, which reminded him of the flowers he'd brought for her. It wasn't at all how Scarlett normally smelled.

Something was seriously wrong.

He scrutinized her face. Eyes, chocolate-brown and fathomless. Same as before. Hair, thick and glossy as mink's fur. Her lips, however, were different. More ripe, more lush and incredibly kissable.

He didn't stop to think and simply reacted. The next instant, his mouth covered hers.

She squirmed and squealed and wrestled him. Hot coffee splashed onto his chest and down his slacks. He let her go, but not because of any pain.

"Are you crazy?" she demanded, her breath coming fast.

Holding on to the wrist with the new tattoo, he narrowed his gaze. "Who the hell are you? And don't bother lying, because I know you aren't Scarlett McPhee."

Look for MOST ELIGIBLE SHERIFF *by Cathy McDavid next month from Harlequin® American Romance®!*